BLUEBIRD WINTER

Bluebird Winter

A Spencer-Nyle Co Romance

Linda Howard

OPEN ROAD
INTEGRATED MEDIA
NEW YORK

ISBN: 978-1-5040-8783-4

This edition published in 2024 by Open Road Integrated Media, Inc.
180 Maiden Lane
New York, NY 10038
www.openroadmedia.com

BLUEBIRD WINTER

Chapter One

It wasn't supposed to happen like this.

Kathleen Fields pressed her hand to her swollen abdomen, her face drawn and anxious as she looked out the window again at the swirling, wind-blown snow. Visibility was so limited that she couldn't even see the uneven pasture fence no more than fifty yards away. The temperature had plummeted into the teens, and according to the weather report on the radio, this freak Christmas Day blizzard was likely to last the rest of the day and most of the night.

She couldn't wait that long. She was in labor now, almost a month early. Her baby would need medical attention.

Bitterness welled in her as she dropped the curtain and turned back to the small, dim living room, lit only by the fire in the fireplace. The electricity and telephone service had gone out five hours ago. Two hours after that, the dull ache in her back, which had been so constant for weeks that she no longer noticed it, had begun strengthening into something more, then laced around to her distended belly. Only mildly concerned, she had ignored it as false labor; after all, she was still three weeks and five days from her due date. Then, half an hour ago, her water had broken, and there was no longer any doubt: she was in labor.

She was also alone, and stranded. This Christmas snow, so coveted by millions of children, could mean the death of her own child.

Tears burned her eyes. She had stolidly endured a bad marriage and the end of her illusions, faced the reality of being broke, alone and pregnant, of working long hours as a waitress in an effort to keep herself fed and provide a home for this baby, even though she had fiercely resented its existence at the beginning. But then it had begun moving inside her, gentle little flutters at first, then actual kicks and pokes, and it had become reality, a person, a companion. It was *her* baby. She wanted it, wanted to hold it and love it and croon lullabies to it. It was the only person she had left in the world, but now she might lose it, perhaps in punishment for that early resentment. How ironic to carry it all this time, only to lose it on Christmas Day! It was supposed to be a day of hope, faith and promise, but she didn't have any hope left, or much faith in people, and the future promised nothing but an endless procession of bleak days. All she had was herself, and the tiny life inside her that was now in jeopardy.

She could deliver the baby here, without help. It was warm and somehow she would manage to keep the fire going. She would survive, but would the baby? It was premature. It might not be able to breathe properly on its own. Something might be wrong with it.

Or she could try to get to the clinic, fifteen miles distant. It was an easy drive in good weather . . . but the weather wasn't good, and the howling wind had been getting louder. The roads were treacherous and visibility limited. She might not make it, and the effort would cost her her own life, as well as that of her child.

So what? The words echoed in her mind. What did her life

matter, if the baby died? Would she be able to live with herself if she opted to protect herself at the risk of the baby's life? Everything might be all right, but she couldn't take that chance. For the baby's sake, she had to try.

Moving clumsily, she dressed as warmly as she could, layering her clothing until she moved like a waddling pumpkin. She gathered water and blankets, an extra nightgown for herself and clothes for the baby, then, as a last thought, checked the telephone one more time on the off-chance that service might have been restored. Only silence met her ear, and, regretfully, she dropped the receiver.

Taking a deep breath to brace herself, Kathleen opened the back door and was immediately lashed by the icy wind and stinging snow. She ducked her head and struggled against the wind, cautiously making her way down the two ice-coated steps. Her balance wasn't that good anyway, and the wind was beating at her, making her stagger. Halfway across the yard she slipped and fell, but scrambled up so quickly that she barely felt the impact. "I'm sorry, I'm sorry," she breathed to the baby, patting her stomach. The baby had settled low in her belly and wasn't kicking now, but the pressure was increasing. It was hard to walk. Just as she reached the old pickup truck a contraction hit her and she stumbled, falling again. This contraction was stronger than the others, and all she could do was lie helplessly in the snow until it eased, biting her lip to keep from moaning aloud.

Snow was matting her eyelashes when she finally struggled to her feet again and gathered up the articles she had dropped. She was panting. God, please let it be a long labor! she prayed. Please give me time to get to the clinic. She could bear the pain, if the baby would just stay snug and safe inside her until she could get help for it.

A dry sobbing sound reached her ears as she wrenched the truck door open, pitting her strength against that of the wind as it tried to slam the door shut. Clumsily she climbed into the truck, barely fitting her swollen stomach behind the wheel. The wind slammed the door shut without her aid, and for a moment she just sat there, entombed in an icy, white world, because snow covered all the windows. The sobbing sound continued, and finally she realized she was making the noise.

Instantly Kathleen drew herself up. There was nothing to gain by letting herself panic. She had to clear her mind and concentrate on nothing but driving, because her baby's life depended on it. The baby was all she had left. Everything else was gone: her parents; her marriage; her self-confidence; her faith and trust in people. Only the baby was left, and herself. She still had herself. The two of them had each other, and they didn't need anyone else. She would do anything to protect her baby.

Breathing deeply, she forced herself to be calm. With deliberate movements, she inserted the key in the ignition and turned it. The starter turned slowly, and a new fear intruded. Was the battery too cold to generate enough power to start the old motor? But then the motor roared into life, and the truck vibrated beneath her. She sighed in relief and turned on the wipers to clear the snow from the windshield. They beat back and forth, laboring under the icy weight of the packed snow.

It was so cold! Her breath fogged the air, and she was shivering despite the layers of clothing she wore. Her face felt numb. She reached up to touch it and found that she was still covered with snow. Slowly she wiped her face and dusted the flakes from her hair.

The increasing pressure in her lower body made it difficult for her to hold in the clutch, but she wrestled the stubborn gearshift into the proper position and ground her teeth against the pressure as she let out the clutch. The truck moved forward.

Visibility was even worse than she had expected. She could barely make out the fence that ran alongside the road. How easy it would be to run off the road, or to become completely lost in the white nightmare! Creeping along at a snail's pace, Kathleen concentrated on the fence line and tried not to think about the things that could happen.

She was barely a quarter of a mile down the road when another contraction laced her stomach in iron bands. She gasped, jerking in spite of herself, and the sudden wrench of the steering wheel sent the old truck into a skid. "No!" she groaned, bracing herself as the truck began going sideways toward the shallow ditch alongside the road. The two right wheels landed in the ditch with an impact that rattled her teeth and loosened her grip from the steering wheel. She cried out again as she was flung to the right, her body slamming into the door on the passenger side.

The contraction eased a moment later. Panting, Kathleen crawled up the slanting seat and wedged herself behind the steering wheel. The motor had died, and anxiously she put in the clutch and slid the shift into neutral, praying she could get the engine started again. She turned the key, and once again the truck coughed into life.

But the wheels spun uselessly in the icy ditch, unable to find traction. She tried rocking the truck back and forth, putting it first in reverse, then in low gear, but it didn't work. She was stuck.

Tiredly, she leaned her head on the steering wheel. She was only a quarter of a mile from the house, but it might as well have been twenty miles in this weather. The wind was stronger, visibility almost zero. Her situation had gone from bad to worse. She should have stayed at the house. In trying to save her baby, she had almost certainly taken away its only chance for survival.

He should either have left his mother's house the day before, or remained until the roads were clear. Hindsight was, indeed, very sharp, unlike the current visibility. His four-wheel-drive Jeep Cherokee was surefooted on the icy road, but that didn't eliminate the need to see where he was going.

Making a mistake made Derek Taliferro angry, especially when it was such a stupid mistake. Yesterday's weather bulletins had warned that conditions could worsen, so he had decided to make the drive back to Dallas right away. But Marcie had wanted him to stay until Christmas morning, and he loved his mother very much, so in the end he'd stayed. His strong mouth softened as he allowed himself to think briefly of her. She was a strong woman, raising him single-handedly and never letting him think she'd have it any other way. He'd been elated when she had met Whit Campbell, a strong, laconic rancher from Oklahoma, and tumbled head over heels in love. That had been . . . Lord, ten years ago. It didn't seem that long. Marcie and Whit still acted like newlyweds.

Derek liked visiting the ranch, just across the state line in Oklahoma, and escaping the pressures of the hospital for a while. That was one reason he'd allowed Marcie to talk him into staying longer than his common sense told him he should. But this morning the urge to get back to Dallas had also overridden his common sense. He should have stayed put until the weather cleared, but he wanted to be back at the hospital by tomorrow. His tiny patients needed him.

The job was compelling, and he never tired of it. He had known he wanted to be a doctor from the time he was fifteen, but at first he'd thought about being an obstetrician. Gradually his interest had become more focused, and by the time he was midway through medical school his goal was set. He specialized in neonatal care, in those tiny babies who came into the world with less of a chance than they should have had. Some of them were simply premature and needed a protective environment in which to gain weight. Others, who were far too early, had to fight for every breath as their underdeveloped systems tried to mature. Every day was a battle won. Then there were those who needed his surgical skills after nature had gone awry, and still others who were beyond help. Every time he was finally able to send a baby home with its parents, he was filled with an intense satisfaction that showed no signs of lessening. It was also why he was now creeping, almost blindly, through a blizzard instead of waiting for better weather. He wanted to get back to the hospital.

The snow completely covered the road; he'd been following the fence lines, and hoping he was still on track. Hell, for all he knew, he was driving across someone's pasture. This was idiocy. He swore under his breath, holding the Cherokee steady against the gusting, howling, swirling wind. When he got to the next town—*if* he got to the next town—he was going to stop, even if he had to spend the night in an all-night grocery . . . provided there was an all-night grocery. Anything was better than driving blindly in this white hell.

It was so bad that he almost missed seeing the bulk of an old pickup truck, which had slid into a ditch and was now resting at an angle. In one sense seeing the old truck was good news: at least he was still on the road. He started to go on, thinking that whoever had been driving the truck would have sought more adequate shelter long ago, but a quick uneasy feeling made him brake carefully, then shift into reverse and back up until he was alongside the snow-covered bulk. It would only take a minute to check.

The snow had turned into icy, wind-driven pellets that stung his face as he opened the door and got out, hunching his broad shoulders against the wind that tried to knock him off his feet. It was only a few steps to the truck, but he had to fight for every inch. Quickly he grabbed the door handle and wrenched it open, wanting to verify that the truck was empty so he could get back into the Cherokee's warm interior. He was startled by the small scream from the woman who lay on the seat and then jerked upright in alarm when the door was opened so suddenly.

"I just want to help," he said quickly, to keep from frightening her more than he already had.

Kathleen gasped, panting at the pain that had her in its grips. The contractions had been intensifying and were only a few minutes apart now. She would never have been able to make it to the clinic in time. She felt the numbing blast of cold, saw the big man who stood in the truck's open door; but just for the moment she couldn't reply, couldn't do anything except concentrate on the pain. She wrapped her arms around her tight belly, whimpering.

Derek realized at a glance what was happening. The woman was completely white, her green eyes vivid in her pale, desperate face as she held her swollen belly. A strong sense of protectiveness surged through him.

"It's all right, sweetheart," he murmured soothingly, reaching into the truck and lifting her out in his strong arms. "You and the baby will be just fine. I'll take care of everything."

She was still whimpering, locked in the grip of the contraction. Derek carried her to the Cherokee, sheltering her from the brutal wind as much as he could. His mind was already on the coming birth. He hadn't delivered a baby since he'd been an

10

intern, but he'd been on hand many times when the newborn was expected to have difficulties.

He managed to open the passenger door with her still in his arms, and gently deposited her on the seat before hurrying around to vault in on his own side. "How far apart are the contractions?" he asked, wiping her face with his hands. She lay slumped against the seat now, breathing deeply at the cessation of pain, her eyelids closed.

Her eyes opened at his touch, the wary eyes of a wild animal in a trap. "Th-th-th-three minutes," she said, her teeth chattering from the cold. "Maybe less."

"How far is the hospital?"

"Clinic," she corrected, still breathing hard. She swallowed and wet her lips. "Fifteen miles."

"We won't make it," he said with awful certainty. "Is there anyplace around here where we can shelter? A house, a restaurant, anything?"

She lifted her hand. "My house . . . back there. Quarter mile."

Derek's experienced eyes took note of the signs. She was exhausted. Labor was tiring enough, without being alone and terrified, too. Stress had taken its toll. He needed to get her warm and comfortable as soon as possible. Her eyes closed again.

He decided not to chance turning the truck around and getting off the road; instead he put the Cherokee in reverse, guiding himself by the fence line beside him, because he couldn't see a damned thing out the back window. "Tell me when I get to your driveway," he ordered, and her eyes fluttered open in response.

A minute or so later another contraction curled her in the seat. Derek glanced at his watch. Just a little over two minutes since the last one. The baby certainly wasn't waiting for better weather.

A rusted mailbox on a leaning fence post caught his attention. "Is this your driveway?" he asked.

She lifted her head, and he could see that her white teeth were sunk into her bottom lip to hold back her groans. She managed a short nod, and he shifted into low gear, turning onto the faint trail by the mailbox and praying for time.

Chapter Two

"The back door's open," Kathleen whispered, and he nodded as he steered the Cherokee as close to the steps as he could.

"Don't try to get out on your own," he ordered as she reached for the door handle. "I'll come around and get you."

Kathleen subsided against the seat, her face pale and taut. She didn't know this man, didn't know whether she should trust him, but she had no choice but to accept his help. She was more frightened than she'd ever been in her life. The pain was worse than she'd expected, and added to it was the numbing fear for her child's life. Whoever the man was, right now she was grateful for his company.

He got out of the Cherokee, bending his head against the wind as he circled the front of the vehicle. He was a big man, tall and strong; he'd handled her weight easily, but his grasp had been gentle. As he opened the passenger door, Kathleen started to swing her legs around so she could slide out, but again he stopped her by scooping her up in his arms.

"Put your face against my shoulder," he instructed, raising his voice so she could hear him over the howling wind. She nodded and buried her face against his coat, and he turned so that his back blocked the wind from her as he carried her the few feet to the back door. He fumbled for the doorknob and managed to turn it, and the wind did the rest, catching the door and slamming it back against the wall with a resounding crack. A small blizzard of snow entered with them.

Swiftly he carried her through the small, time-worn ranch house until he reached the living room, where the fire still burned low in the fireplace. She felt as though hours had passed, but in reality it had been only about an hour since she had fought her way to the truck.

Still with that powerful, controlled gentleness, he placed her on the sagging old couch. "I've got to get my bag, but I'll be right back," he promised, smoothing her hair back from her face. "Don't try to get up; stay right here."

She nodded, so tired that she couldn't imagine going anywhere. Why did he want his luggage right now? Couldn't it wait?

Another contraction. She curled up on the couch, giving gasping little cries at the fierceness of the pain. Before it ended he was beside her again, his voice soothing but authoritative as he told her to take quick, short breaths, to pant like a dog. Dimly she remembered reading instructions for breathing during labor, and the same description had been used. She tried to do as he said, concentrating on her breathing, and it did seem to help. Perhaps it just took her mind off the pain, but right then she was willing to do anything.

When the contraction had eased and she slumped exhausted on the couch, he said, "Do you have extra wood for the fire? The electricity is off."

She managed a wan smile. "I know. It went off this morning. I brought extra wood in yesterday, when I heard the weather report; it's in the wash room, just off the kitchen."

"You should have gone to the clinic yesterday," he said crisply as he got to his feet.

She was tired and frightened, but fire still flashed in her green eyes as she glared up at him. "I would have, if I'd known the baby was going to come early."

That got his attention; his black brows snapped together over his high-bridged nose. "You're not full term? How early are you?"

"Almost a month." Her hand went to her stomach in an unconscious gesture of helpless concern.

"Any chance your due date was miscalculated?"

"No," she whispered, her head falling back. She knew exactly when she'd gotten pregnant, and the memory made her go cold.

He gave her a crooked smile, and for the first time she noticed how beautiful he was, in a strong, masculine way that was almost unearthly. Kathleen had gotten into the habit of not looking directly at men, or she would have seen it before. Even now, something in his golden brown eyes made her feel more relaxed. "This is your lucky day, sweetheart," he said gently, still smiling at her as he took off his thick shearling coat and rolled up his sleeves. "You just got stranded with a doctor."

For a moment the words didn't make sense; then her mouth opened in silent disbelief. "You're a doctor?"

He lifted his right hand as if taking an oath. "Licensed and sworn."

Relief filled her like a warm tide rushing through her body, and she gave a small laugh that was half sob. "Are you any good at delivering babies?"

"Babies are my business," he said, giving her another of those bright, tender smiles. "So stop worrying and try to rest while I get things arranged in here. When you have another contraction, remember how to breathe. I won't be long."

She watched as he brought in more wood and built up the fire until it was blazing wildly, adding warmth to the chilled room. Through the pain of another contraction, she watched as he carried in the mattress from her bed and dumped it on the floor in front of the fire. With swift, sure movements he put a clean sheet on it, then folded towels over the sheet.

He rose to his feet with powerful grace and approached her. "Now, let's get you more comfortable," he said as he removed her coat. "By the way, my name is Derek Taliferro."

"Kathleen Fields," she replied in kind.

"Is there a Mr. Fields?" he asked, his calm face hiding his intense interest in her as he began taking off her boots.

Bitterness filled Kathleen's face, a bitterness so deep it hurt to see. "There's one somewhere," she muttered. "But we aren't married any longer."

He was silent as he removed her thick socks, under which she also wore leotards that she'd put on when she realized she would have to try to get to the clinic. He helped her to her feet and unzipped her serviceable corduroy jumper, lifting it over her head and leaving her standing in the turtleneck sweater and leotards.

"I can do the rest," she said uneasily. "Just let me go into the bedroom for a nightgown."

He laughed, the sound deep and rich. "All right, if you think you can manage."

"Of course I can manage." She had been managing much more than that since Larry Fields had walked out.

But she had barely taken two steps when another contraction bent her double, a contraction so powerful that it was all she could do to gasp for breath. Involuntary tears stung her eyes. She felt his arms around her; then he lifted her and a moment later placed her on the mattress. Swiftly he stripped off her leotards and underwear, and draped a sheet over her; then he held her hand and coached her breathing until the contraction eased.

"Rest for a minute now," he soothed. "I'm going to wash my hands so I can examine you. I'll be right back."

Kathleen lay tiredly on the mattress, staring up at the water-stained ceiling with swimming eyes. The heat from the fire flickered against her cheeks, bringing a rosy glow to her complexion. She was so tired; she felt as if she could sleep for the rest of the day, but there wouldn't be any rest until the baby was born. Her hands clenched into fists as anxiety rose in her again. The baby had to be all right. It had to be.

Then he was back, kneeling at the foot of the mattress and lifting the sheet that covered her. Real color climbed into her face, and she turned her head to stare into the fire. She had never really been comfortable with intimacy, and even her visits to the doctor had been torturous occasions for her. To have this man, this stranger, touch her and look at her . . .

Derek glanced up and saw her flushed face and expression of acute embarrassment, and a smile flickered around his mouth as amused tenderness welled up in him. How wary she was of him, despite being forced to put her welfare in his hands! And rather shy, like a wild creature that wasn't accustomed to others and didn't quite trust them. She was frightened, too, for her child, and of the ordeal she faced. Because of that, he was immensely gentle as he examined her.

"You aren't fully dilated," he murmured. "The baby isn't in such a hurry, after all. Go with your contractions, but don't push. I'll tell you when to push. How long ago did the contractions start?"

"My back was hurting all last night," she said tiredly, her eyes closing. "The first real contraction was at about ten o'clock this morning."

He glanced at his watch. She had been in labor a little over five hours, and it would probably last another hour or so. Not a long labor, especially for a first pregnancy. "When did your water break?"

He wasn't hurting her, and her embarrassment was fading. She even felt drowsy. "Umm . . . about one-thirty." Now she felt his hands on her stomach; firm, careful touches as he tried to determine the baby's position. Her warm drowsiness splintered as another contraction seized her, but when she breathed as he'd instructed somehow it didn't seem as painful.

When she rested again, he placed his stethoscope against her stomach and listened to the baby's heartbeat. "It's a strong, steady hearbeat," he reassured her. He wasn't worried about the baby's heart, but about its lungs. He prayed they would be mature enough to handle the chore of breathing, because he didn't have the equipment here to handle the situation if they couldn't. Some eight-month babies did just fine; others needed help. He looked out the window. It was snowing harder than ever, in a blinding sheet that blocked out the rest of the world but filled the house with a strange, white light. There was no way he could summon emergency help, and no way it could get here, even if the phones were working.

The minutes slipped away, marked by contractions that gradually grew stronger and closer together. He kept the fire built up, so the baby wouldn't be chilled when it finally made its appearance, and Kathleen's hair grew damp with sweat. She tugged at the neck of her turtleneck sweater. "It's so hot," she breathed. She felt as if she couldn't stand the confining fabric a minute longer.

"A nightgown wouldn't be much of an improvement," Derek said, and got one of his clean shirts from his luggage. She didn't make any protest when he removed her sweater and bra and slipped the thin, soft shirt around her. It was light, and much too big, and it felt wonderful after the smothering heat of the wool sweater. He rolled up the sleeves and fastened the buttons over her breasts, then dampened a washcloth in cool water and bathed her face.

It wouldn't be too much longer. He checked again to make certain he had everything he needed at hand. He had already sterilized his instruments and laid everything out on a gauze-covered tray.

"Well, sweetheart, are you about ready to get this show on the road?" he asked as he examined her again.

The contractions were almost continuous now. She took a deep breath during a momentary lull. "Is it time?" she gasped.

"You're fully dilated now, but don't push until I tell you. Pant. That's right. Don't push, don't push."

She wanted to push. She desperately needed to push. Her body arched on the mattress, a monstrous pressure building in her, but his deep voice remained calm and controlled, somehow controlling her. She panted, and somehow, she didn't push. The wave of pain receded, the pressure eased, and for a moment she rested. Then it began again.

It couldn't last much longer; she couldn't bear it much longer. Tears seeped from her eyes.

"Here we go," he said with satisfaction. "I can see the head. You're crowning, sweetheart; it won't be but another minute. Let me make a little incision so you won't be torn—"

Kathleen barely heard him, barely felt him. The pressure was unbearable, blocking out everything else. "Push, sweetheart," he said, his tone suddenly authoritative.

She pushed. Dimly, she was astounded that her body was capable of exerting such pressure. She gave a thin cry, but barely heard it. Her world consisted only of a powerful force that squeezed her in its fist, that and the man who knelt at her spread knees, his calm voice telling her what to do.

Then, abruptly, the pressure eased, and she sank back, gasping for breath. He said, "I have the baby's head in my hand. My Lord, what a head of hair! Just rest a minute, sweetheart."

She heard a funny sound, and alarm brought her up on her elbows. "What's wrong?" she asked frantically. "What are you doing?"

"I'm suctioning out its mouth and nose," he said. "Just lie back; everything's all right." Then a thin, wavering wail rose, gaining in strength with every second, and he laughed. "That's right, tell us about it," he encouraged. "Push, sweetheart; our baby isn't too happy with the situation."

She pushed, straining, and suddenly she felt a rush, then a great sense of relief. Derek laughed again as he held a tiny but furious scrap of humanity in his hands. "I don't blame you a bit," he told the squalling infant, whose cries sounded ridiculously like those of a mewling kitten. "I wouldn't want to leave your soft, warm mommy, either, but you'll be wrapped up and cuddled in just a minute."

"What is it?" Kathleen whispered, falling back on the mattress.

"A beautiful little girl. She has more hair than any three babies should have."

"Is she all right?"

"She's perfect. She's tiny, but listen to her cry! Her lungs are working just fine."

"Can I hold her?"

"In just a minute. I'm almost finished here." The umbilical cord had gone limp, so he swiftly clamped and cut it, then lifted the squalling baby into her mother's anxious arms. Kathleen looked dazed, her eyes filling with tears as she examined her tiny daughter.

"Put her to your breast," Derek instructed softly, knowing that would calm the infant, but Kathleen didn't seem to hear him. He unbuttoned her shirt himself and pushed it aside to bare one full breast, then guided the baby's mouth to the rich-looking nipple. Still the baby squalled, its tiny body trembling; he'd have to do more than just give it a hint. "Come on, honey," he coaxed, reached down to stroke the baby's cheek just beside her mouth. She turned her head reflexively, and he guided the nipple into her mouth. She squalled one more time, then suddenly seemed to realize what she was supposed to do, and the tiny mouth closed on her mother's breast.

Kathleen jumped. She hadn't even reacted to his touch on her breast, he realized, and looked closely at her. She was pale, with shadows under her eyes, and her dark hair was wet with perspiration. She was truly exhausted, not just from the physical difficulty of labor and giving birth, but from the hours of anxiety she'd suffered through. Yet there was something glowing in her face and eyes as she looked at her baby, and it lingered when she slowly looked up at him.

"We did it," she murmured, and smiled.

Derek looked down at her, at the love shining from her face like a beacon, and the attraction he'd felt for her from the start suddenly solidified inside him with a painful twist. Something about her made him want to hold her close, protect her from whatever had put that wary, distrustful look in her eyes. He wanted her to look at him with her face full of love.

Stunned, he sank back on his heels. It had finally happened, when he had least expected it and had even stopped looking for it, and with a woman who was merely tolerating his presence due to the circumstances. It wasn't just that she had other things on her mind right now; he could tell that Kathleen Fields wanted nothing to do with a man, any man. And yet the thunderbolt had hit him anyway, just as his mother had always warned him it would.

Teaching Kathleen to love wouldn't be easy, but Derek looked at her, and at the baby in her arms, and knew he wouldn't give up.

Chapter Three

Kathleen couldn't remember ever being so tired before; her body was leaden with exhaustion, while her mind seemed to float, disconnected from the physical world. Only the baby in her arms seemed real. She was vaguely aware of the things Derek was doing to her, of the incredible confidence and gentleness of his hands, but it was as if he were doing them to someone else. Even the painful prick of the sutures he set didn't rouse her, nor did his firm massaging of her stomach. She simply lay there, too tired to care. When she was finally clean and wearing a gown, and the linen on the mattress had been changed, she sighed and went to sleep with the suddenness of a light being turned off.

She had no idea how long it was before he woke her, to lift her carefully to a sitting position and prop her against him while the baby nursed. He was literally holding both her and the baby, his strong arms supporting them. Her head lay on his broad shoulder, and she didn't have the strength to lift it. "I'm sorry," she murmured. "I can't seem to sit up."

"It's all right, sweetheart," he said, his deep voice reaching inside her and soothing all her vague worries. "You worked hard; you deserve to be a little lazy now."

"Is the baby all right?" she managed to mumble.

"She's eating like a pig," he said, his chuckle hiding his worry, and Kathleen went back to sleep as soon as he eased her back onto the mattress. She didn't even feel him lift the baby from her and refasten her gown.

Derek sat for a long time, cradling the baby in his arms. She was dangerously underweight, but she seemed remarkably strong for her size. She was breathing on her own and managing to suckle, which had been his two biggest worries, but she was still too tiny. He guessed her weight at about four pounds, too small for her to be able to regulate her own temperature because she simply didn't have the body fat necessary. Because of that, he had wrapped her warmly and kept the fire in the fireplace hotter than was comfortable.

His calm, golden brown eyes glowed as he looked down at her tiny face, dominated by the vague, huge blue eyes of the newborn. Premature infants had both an aged and a curiously ageless look to them, their doll-like faces lacking cuddly baby fat, which revealed their facial structure in a fragile gauntness. Even so, he could tell she was going to be a beauty, with her mother's features and even the same thick, black hair.

Every one of his tiny, frail patients got to him, but this stubborn little fighter had reached into his heart. Maybe it was because he could look at her and see her mother in her, because Kathleen was a fighter, too. She had to be; it wasn't easy to go through a pregnancy alone, as she obviously had. And when she had gone into labor too early, instead of remaining here where *she* would be safer, she had risked her own life in an effort to get to the clinic where her baby could have medical care.

He couldn't help wondering about the absent Mr. Fields, and for the first time in his life he felt jealousy burning him, because the unknown man had been, at least for a while, the recipient of Kathleen's love. Derek also wondered what had happened to put that wariness in her eyes and build the walls in her mind. He knew they were there; he could sense them. They made him want to put his arms around her and rock her, comfort her, but he knew she wouldn't welcome his closeness.

The baby squeaked, and he looked down to see that her eyes were open and she was looking at him with the intensely focused expression of someone with bad eyesight. He chuckled and cuddled her closer. "What is it, honey?" he crooned. "Hungry again?" Because her stomach was so small, she needed far more frequent feedings than a normal newborn.

He glanced over at Kathleen, who was still sleeping heavily. An idea began to form. One of Derek's characteristics, and one that had often made his mother feel as if she were dealing with an irresistible force rather than a child, was his ability to set long-term goals and let nothing sway him from his course. When he wanted something, he went after it. And now he wanted Kathleen. He had been instantly attracted to her, his interest sparked by the mysterious but undeniable chemical reaction that kept animals mating and procreating; humans were no exception, and his own libido was healthy. Her pregnancy hadn't weakened his attraction, but rather strengthened it in a primitive way.

Then, during the process of labor and giving birth, the attraction had changed, had been transmitted into an emotional force as well as a physical one. They had been a team, despite Kathleen's reserve. The baby had become his; he was responsible for her life, her welfare. She had exited her mother's warm body into his hands. He had seen her, held her, laughed at her furious squalling, and put her to her mother's breast. She was, undeniably, *his*. Now his goal was to make the baby's mother his, too. He wanted Kathleen to look at him with the same fiercely tender love she'd shown to her child. He wanted to father the next infant that grew inside her. He wanted to make her laugh, to ease the distrust in her eyes, to make her face shine with happiness.

No doubt about it, he'd have to marry her.

The baby squeaked again, more demandingly. "All right, we'll wake Mommy up," he promised. "You'll help with my plan, won't you? Between the two of us, we'll take such good care of her that she'll forget she was ever unhappy."

He woke Kathleen before the baby began to squall in earnest, and carefully propped her in a sitting position so she could nurse the child. She was still groggy, but seemed more alert than she had before. She held the baby to her breast, stroking the satiny cheek with one finger as she stared down at her daughter. "What time is it?" she asked dreamily.

He shifted his position so he could see his wristwatch. "Almost nine."

"Is that all? I feel as if I've been asleep for hours."

He laughed. "You have, sweetheart. You were worn out."

Kathleen's clear green eyes turned up to him. "Is she doing all right?"

The baby chose that moment to slurp as the nipple momentarily slipped from her lips. Frantically the tiny rosebud mouth sought the beading nipple again, and when she found it she made a squeaky little grunting noise. The two adults laughed, looking down at her.

"She's strong for her size," Derek said, reaching down to lift the miniscule hand that lay on Kathleen's ivory, blue-veined breast. It was such a tiny hand, the palm no bigger than a dime, but the fingernails were perfectly formed and a nice pink color. Sweat trickled at his temple, and he could see a fine sheen on Kathleen's chest, but at least the baby was warm enough.

Kathleen tried to sit up away from him, her eyes sharpening

as she considered his reply, but her body protested the movement, and with a quiet moan she sank back against his muscled chest. "What do you mean, she's strong for her size? Is she doing all right or not?"

"She needs an incubator," he said, wrapping his arm around Kathleen and supporting her soft weight. "That's why I'm keeping it so hot in here. She's too small for her body to regulate its own temperature."

Kathleen's face was suddenly white and tense. She had thought everything was fine, despite the baby being a month early. The sudden knowledge that the baby was still in a precarious position stunned her.

"Don't worry," Derek soothed, cradling her close to him. "As long as we keep her nice and warm, she shouldn't have any trouble. I'll keep a close watch on her tonight, and as soon as the weather clears we'll get her to a cozy incubator." He studied the fragile little hand for a moment longer, then tenderly replaced it on Kathleen's breast. "What are you going to name her?"

"Sara Marisa," Kathleen murmured. "Sara is—was—my mother's name. But I'm going to call her Risa. It means 'laughter.'"

Derek's face went still, and his eyes darkened with barely contained emotion as he looked at the baby. "How are you spelling it? S-a-r-a or S-a-r-a-h?"

"S-a-r-a."

It was still the same name, the name that had become synonymous, in his mind, with love. He had first seen mind-shattering, irrevocable love in Sarah Matthews's face when he had been fifteen, and he had known then that he would never settle for anything less. That was what he wanted to feel, what he wanted to give, what he wanted in return. Sarah's love was a powerful, immense thing, spilling over into the lives of everyone near her, because she gave it so unselfishly. It was because of her that he was a doctor now, because of her that he had been able to finish college at an accelerated pace, because of her that he had a warm, loving extended family when before there had been only himself and his mother. Now this new life was leading him into the sort of love he'd waited for, so it was only fitting that she should be named Sara. He smiled when he thought of Sara holding her namesake. She and her husband, Rome, could be the baby's godparents, though they'd probably have to share the honor with Max and Claire Conroy, two other very special friends and part of the extended family. He knew how they would all take to Kathleen and the baby, but he wondered how Kathleen would feel, surrounded by all those loving strangers. Anxious? Threatened?

It would take time to teach Kathleen to love him, and all the people who were close to him, but he had all the time in the world. He had the rest of his life.

The baby was asleep now, and gently he took her from Kathleen's arms. "Risa," he murmured, trying her name on his tongue. Yes, the two of them together would overwhelm Kathleen with love.

Kathleen dozed on and off the rest of the night, and every time she woke she saw Derek with her daughter in his arms. The picture of the tall, strong man holding the frail infant with such tender concern gave her a feeling she couldn't identify, as if something expanded in her chest. He didn't let down his guard for a minute all night, but kept vigil over the child, kept the room uncomfortably warm, and held Kathleen so she could nurse her whenever that funny, indignant little squeak told them the baby was getting hungry. Sometime during the night he removed his shirt, and when she woke the next time she was stunned by the primitive beauty of the picture he made, sitting cross-legged before the fire, the powerful muscles of his damp torso gleaming as he cuddled the sleeping baby to him.

It struck her then that he wasn't like other men, but she was too sleepy and too tired to pursue the thought. Her entire body ached, and she was in the grip of a powerful lassitude that kept her thoughts and movements down to a minimum. Tomorrow would be time enough to think.

It stopped snowing around dawn, and the wild, whistling wind died away. It was the pale silence that woke her for good, and she gingerly eased herself into a sitting position, wincing at the pain in her lower body. Derek laid the baby on the mattress and reached out a strong arm to help her.

"I have to go—" she began, stopping abruptly as she wondered how she could phrase the urgent need to a stranger.

"It's about time," he said equably, carefully lifting her in his arms.

Her face turned scarlet as he carried her down the dark, narrow hallway. "I don't need any help!" she protested.

He set her on her feet outside the bathroom door and held her until her legs stopped wobbling. "I put a couple of candles in here last night," he said. "I'll light them, then *get* out of your way, but I'll be just outside the door if you need me."

She realized that he didn't intend to embarrass her, but neither was he going to let her do more than he deemed wise. There was a calm implacability in his face that told her he wouldn't hesitate to come to her aid if she became too weak to take care of herself. It was difficult to remember that he was a doctor, used to bodies of all sizes and shapes. He just didn't seem like any doctor she'd ever met before.

To her relief, her strength was returning, and she didn't need his help. When she left the bathroom, she walked down the hall under her own power, though he kept a steadying hand under her arm just in case. The baby was still sleeping peacefully on the mattress, and Kathleen looked down at her daughter with a powerful surge of adoration that shook her.

"She's so beautiful," she whispered. "Is she doing okay?"

"She's doing fine, but she needs an incubator until she gains about a pound and a half. The way she's been nursing, that might take only a couple of weeks."

"A couple of weeks!" Kathleen echoed, aghast. "She needs hospital care for a couple of weeks?"

His eyes were steady. "Yes."

Kathleen turned away, her fists knotting. There was no way she could pay what two weeks in a hospital would cost, yet she couldn't see that she had a choice. Risa's life was still a fragile thing, and she would do anything, anything at all, to keep her child alive.

"Does the clinic that you were going to have the facilities to care for her?" he asked.

Another problem. She swallowed. "No. I . . . I don't have any medical insurance. I was going to have her there, then come home afterward."

"Don't worry about it," he said. "I'll think of something. Now, sweetheart, lie down and let me take a look at you. I want to make sure *you're* doing all right."

It had been bad enough the day before, when she was in labor, but it was worse now. It had been a medical emergency then; now it wasn't. But, again, she had the feeling he would do exactly as he intended, regardless of any objections she raised, so she stared fixedly at the fire as he examined her and firmly kneaded her abdomen.

"You have good muscle tone," he said approvingly. "You'd have had a lot harder time if you hadn't been as strong as you are."

If she was strong, it was the strength given by years of

working a small grubby ranch, then long hours of waiting on tables. Spas and gyms were outside her experience.

"What do we do now?" she asked. "Wait?"

"Nope. You're doing well enough to travel, and we can't afford to sit around until the phones are fixed. I'm going to start the Jeep and get it warm, and then I'm taking both you and the baby to a hospital."

She felt instant panic. "You want to take the baby *out*?"

"We have to. We'll keep her warm."

"We can keep her warm here."

"She needs a hospital. She's doing all right now, but things can change in the blink of an eye with a preemie. I'm not going to take that chance with her life."

Kathleen couldn't control a mother's natural fear of exposing her fragile child to the elements. There was no telling which roads were closed, or how long it would take them to reach a hospital. What if they ran off the road again and got in a wreck?

Seeing her panic build, Derek reached out and firmly took her hand. "I won't let anything happen," he said calmly, as if he had read her thoughts. "Get dressed while I start the Jeep and fix something for breakfast. Aren't you hungry? You haven't eaten a bite since I found you yesterday."

Only then did she realize how empty she was; it was odd, how even the thought of hunger had been pushed from her mind by all that happened. She changed in her icy bedroom, hurriedly pulling on first one pair of pants after another, and growing more and more frustrated as she found that they were too small. Finally she settled on one of the first pairs of maternity pants she had bought, when she had been outgrowing her jeans. Her own body was unfamiliar to her. It felt strange not to have a swollen, cumbersome stomach, strange to actually look down and see her toes. She had to move carefully, but she could put on socks and shoes without twisting into awkward contortions. Still, she didn't have her former slenderness, and it was disconcerting.

After pulling on a white cotton shirt and layering a flannel shirt over it, she pulled a brush through her tangled hair and left the bedroom, too cold to linger and worry about her looks. Wryly, she admitted that he had successfully distracted her from her arguments; she had done exactly as he'd ordered.

When she entered the kitchen, he looked up from his capable preparations of soup and sandwiches to smile at her. "Feel strange not wearing maternity clothes?"

"I am wearing maternity clothes," she said, a faint, very feminine despair in her eyes and voice. "What feels strange is being able to see my feet." Changing the subject, she asked, "Is it terribly cold outside?"

"It's about twenty degrees, but the sky is clearing."

"What hospital are you taking us to?"

"I've thought about that. I want Risa in my hospital in Dallas."

"Dallas! But that's—"

"I can oversee her care there," Derek interrupted calmly.

"It's too far away," Kathleen said, standing straight. Her green eyes were full of bitter acknowledgement. "And I won't be able to pay. Just take us to a charity hospital."

"Don't worry about paying. I told you I'd take care of you."

"It's still charity, but I'd rather owe a hospital than you."

"You won't owe me." He turned from the old wood stove, and suddenly she felt the full force of his golden brown gaze, fierce and compelling, bending her to his will. "Not if you marry me."

Chapter Four

The words resounded in her head like the ringing of a bell. "Marry you?"

"That's right."

"But . . . *why*?"

"You'll marry me so Risa can have the care she needs. I'll marry you so I can have Risa. You're not in love with someone, are you?" Numbly she shook her head. "I didn't think so. I guess I fell in love with your daughter the minute she came out of you, into my hands. I want to be her father."

"I don't want to get married again, ever!"

"Not even for Risa? If you marry me, you won't have to worry about money again. I'll sign a prenuptial agreement, if you'd like; I'll provide for her, put her through college."

"You can't marry me just because you want my baby. Get married to someone else and have your own children."

"I want Risa," he said with that calm, frightening implacability. Alarm began to fill her as she realized that he never swerved from the course he had set for himself.

"Think, Kathleen. She needs help now, and children need a lot of support through the years. Am I such a monster that you can't stand the thought of being married to me?"

"But you're a stranger! I don't know you and you don't know me. How can you even think of marrying me?"

"I know that you loved your child enough to risk your own life trying to get to the clinic. I know you've had some bad luck in your life, but that you're strong, and you don't give up. We delivered a baby together; how can we be strangers now?"

"I don't know anything about your life."

He shrugged his broad shoulders. "I have a fairly uncomplicated life. I'm a doctor, I live in an apartment, and I'm not a social lion. I'm great with kids, and I won't mistreat you."

"I never thought you would," she said quietly. She had been mistreated, and she knew that Derek was as different from her ex-husband as day was from night. But she simply didn't want another man in her life at all, ever. "What if you fall in love with someone else? Wouldn't that tear Risa's life apart? I'd never give up custody of her!"

"I won't fall in love with anybody else." His voice rang with utter certainty. He just stood there, watching her, but his eyes were working their power on her. Incredibly, she could feel herself weakening inside. As his wife, she wouldn't have the bitter, day after day after day struggle simply to survive. Risa would have the hospital care she needed, and afterward she would have all the advantages Kathleen couldn't give her.

"I couldn't . . . I couldn't have sex with you," she finally said in desperation, because it was her last defense.

"I wouldn't want you to." Before she could decide if she should feel relieved or insulted, he continued, "When we sleep together, I want you to think of it as making love, not having sex. Sex is cheap and easy. Making love means caring and commitment."

"And you think we'll have that?"

"In time." He gave her a completely peaceful smile, as if he sensed her weakening and knew he would have things his way.

Her throat grew tight as she thought about having sex. She didn't know what making love was, and she didn't know if she would ever *want* to know. "Things . . . have happened to me," she said hoarsely. "I may not ever—"

"In time, sweetheart. You will, in time."

His very certainty frightened her, because there was something about him that abruptly made her just as certain that, at some point in the future, she would indeed want him to make love to her. The idea was alien to her, making her feel as if her entire life had suddenly been rerouted onto another track. She had had everything planned in her mind: she would raise Risa, totally devoted to her only child, and take pleasure in watching her grow. But there was no room for a man in her plans. Larry Fields had done her a tremendous favor by leaving her, even if he had left her broke and pregnant. But now, here was this man who looked like a warrior angel, taking over her life and shaping it along other lines.

Desperately she tried again. "We're too different! You're a doctor, and I barely finished high school. I've lived on this scrubby little ranch my entire life. I've never been anywhere or done anything; you'd be bored to death by me within a month!"

Amusement sparkled in his amber eyes as he walked over to her. "You're talking rubbish," he said gently, his hand sliding under her heavy hair to clasp her nape. Before she could react he had bent and firmly pressed his mouth to hers in a warm, strangely intimate kiss; then he released her and moved away before she could become alarmed. She stood there staring at him, her vivid green eyes huge and confused.

"Say yes, then let's eat," he commanded, his eyes still sparkling.

"Yes." Her voice sounded dazed, even to herself.

"That's a good girl." He put his warm hand on her elbow and led her to the table, then carefully got her seated. She was uncomfortable, but was not in such pain that it killed her appetite. Hungrily they ate chicken noodle soup and toasted cheese sandwiches, washed down with good strong coffee. It wasn't normal breakfast fare, but after not eating for so long, she was delighted with it. Then he insisted that she sit still while he cleaned up the kitchen, something that had never happened to her before. She felt pampered, and dazed by all that had happened and she had agreed to.

"I'll pack a few of your clothes and nightgowns, but you won't need much," he said. "Where are the baby's things?"

"In the bottom drawer of my dresser, but some of her clothes are in the truck. I didn't think to get them yesterday when you stopped."

"We'll pick them up on the way. Come into the living room with the baby while I get everything loaded."

She held the sleeping child while he swiftly packed and carried the things out. When he had finished, he brought a tiny, crocheted baby cap that he'd found in the drawer, and put it on Risa's downy head to help keep her warm. Then he wrapped her snugly in several blankets, helped Kathleen into her heavy coat, put the baby in Kathleen's arms, and lifted both of them into his.

"I can walk," she protested, her heart giving a huge leap at being in his arms again. He had kissed her. . . .

"No going up or down steps just yet," he explained. "And no climbing into the Jeep. Keep Risa's face covered."

He was remarkably strong, carrying her with no evident difficulty. His strides were sure as he waded through the snow, avoiding the path he'd already made because it had become icy. Kathleen blinked at the stark whiteness of the landscape. The wind had blown the snow into enormous drifts that almost obliterated the fence line and had piled against the sides of the house and barn. But the air was still and crisp now, the fog of her breath gushing straight out in front of her.

He had turned the heater in the Jeep on high, and it was uncomfortably warm for her. "I'll have to take off this coat," she muttered.

"Wait until we've stopped to get the things out of your truck or you'll get chilled with the door open."

She watched as he went back inside to bank the fires in the fireplace and the wood stove, and to lock the doors. She had lived in this house her entire life, but suddenly she wondered if she'd ever see it again, and if she cared. Her life here hadn't been happy.

Her confusion and hesitancy faded as if they had never been. This place wasn't what she wanted for Risa. For her daughter, she wanted so much more than what she had had. She didn't want Risa to wear patched and faded clothes, to marry out of desperation, or to miss out on the pleasures of life because all her free time was spent on chores.

Derek was taking her away from this, but she wouldn't rely on him. She had made the mistake of relying on a man once before, and she wouldn't do it again. Kathleen decided that as soon as she had recovered from giving birth, and Risa was stronger, she would get a job, save her money, work to better herself. If Derek ever walked away from her as Larry had done, she wouldn't be left stone broke and without the means to support herself. Risa would never have to go hungry or cold.

Five hours later, Kathleen was lying on a snowy-white hospital bed, watching the color television attached to the wall. Her private room was almost luxurious, with a full bath and a pair of comfortable recliners, small oil paintings on the wall, and fresh flowers on her bedside table. The snowstorms hadn't reached as far south as Dallas, and from the window she could see a blue sky only occasionally studded with clouds.

Risa had been whisked away to the neonatal unit, with people jumping to obey Derek's orders. Kathleen herself had been examined by a cheerful obstetrician named Monica Sudley and pronounced in excellent condition. "But I never expected anything different," Dr. Sudley had said casually. "Not with Dr. Taliferro taking care of you."

Dr. Taliferro. Her mind had accepted him as a doctor, but somehow she hadn't really understood it until she had seen him here, in his own milieu, where his deep voice took on a crisp tone of command, and everyone scrambled to satisfy him. She had only seen him wearing jeans and boots and a casual shirt, with his heavy shearling coat, but after arriving at the hospital he had showered and shaved, then changed into the fresh clothes he kept in his office for just such situations. He had seen to Risa, then visited Kathleen to reassure her that the trip hadn't harmed the infant in any way.

He had been the same, yet somehow different. Perhaps it was only the clothes, the dark slacks, white shirt and blue-striped tie, as well as the lab coat he wore over them and the stethoscope around his neck. It was typical doctor's garb, but the effect was jarring. She couldn't help remembering the firelight flickering on his gleaming, muscled shoulders, or the hard, chiseled purity of his profile as he looked down at the child in his arms.

It was also hard to accept the fact that she had agreed to marry him.

Every few hours she put on a robe and walked to the neonatal unit, where Risa was taken out of the incubator and given to her to be fed. The sight of the other frail babies, some of them much smaller than Risa, shook her. They were enclosed in their little glass cubicles with various tubes running into their tiny naked bodies, while little knit caps covered their heads. Thank God Risa was strong enough to nurse!

The first time she fed her daughter, she was led to a rocking chair in a small room away from the other babies, and Risa was brought to her.

"So you're the mother of this little honey," the young nurse said as she laid Risa in Kathleen's eager arms. "She's adorable. I've never seen so much hair on a newborn, and look how long it is! Dr. Taliferro had us scrambling like we were having an air raid until we had her all comfy. Did he really deliver her?"

Faint color burned along Kathleen's cheekbones. Somehow it seemed too intimate to discuss, even though giving birth was an everyday occurrence to the staff. But the young nurse was looking at her with bright, expectant eyes, so she said uncomfortably, "Yes. My truck slid off the road during the blizzard. Derek came by and found me."

"Ohmygod, talk about romantic!"

"Having a baby?" Kathleen asked skeptically.

"Honey, digging ditches would be romantic if Dr. Taliferro helped! Isn't he something? All the babies know whenever he's the one holding them. They never get scared or cry with him. Sometimes he stays here all night with a critical baby, holding it and talking to it, watching it every minute, and a lot of his babies make it when no one else gave them much of a chance."

The nurse seemed to have a case of hero worship for Derek, or maybe it was more than that. He was incredibly good-looking, and a hospital was a hothouse for romances. It made Kathleen uneasy; why was she even thinking of marrying a man who would constantly be pursued and tempted?

"Have you worked in this unit for long?" she asked, trying to change the subject.

"A little over a year. I love it. These little tykes need all the help they can get, and, of course, I'd have walked barefoot over hot coals to get to work with Dr. Taliferro. Hospitals and clinics from all over the nation were fighting to get him."

"Why? Isn't he too young to have built a reputation yet?" She didn't know how old he was, but guessed he was no older than his midthirties, perhaps even younger.

"He's younger than most of them, but he finished college when he was nineteen. He graduated from med school at the top of his class, interned at one of the nation's best trauma centers, then studied neonatal medicine with George Oliver, who's also one of the best. He's thirty-two, I think."

It was odd to learn so much about her future husband from a stranger, and odder still to find he was considered a medical genius, one of those rare doctors whose very name on the staff listing gave a hospital instant credibility. To hide her expression, she looked down at Risa and gently stroked the baby's cheek. "He sat up all night holding Risa," she heard herself say in a strange voice.

The nurse smiled. "He would. And he's still on the floor now, when he should be home sleeping. But that's Dr. Taliferro for you; he puts the babies before himself."

When Kathleen was back in her room, she kept thinking of the things the nurse had told her, and of the things Derek had said to her. He wanted Risa, he'd said. Was that reason enough to marry a woman he didn't love, when he could marry any woman he wanted and have his own children? Of course, he'd also said that eventually he expected to have a normal marriage with her, meaning he intended to sleep with her, so she had to assume he also intended to have children with her. But why was he so certain he'd never fall in love with someone and want out of the marriage?

"Problems?"

The deep, quiet voice startled her, and she looked up to find

Derek standing just inside the door, watching her. She'd been so engrossed in her thoughts that she hadn't heard him.

"No, no problems. I was just . . . thinking."

"Worrying, you mean. Forget about all your second thoughts," he said with disquieting perception. "Just trust me, and let me handle everything. I've made arrangements for us to be married as soon as you're released from the hospital."

"So soon?" she gasped.

"Is there any reason to wait? You'll need a place to live, so you might as well live with me."

"But what about blood tests—"

"The lab here will handle them. When you're released, we'll get our marriage license and go straight to a judge who's an old friend of mine. My apartment is near here, so it'll be convenient for you to come back and forth to feed Risa until she's released. We can use the time to get a nursery set up for her."

She felt helpless. As he'd said, he had handled everything.

Chapter Five

Kathleen felt as if she'd been swept up by a tornado, and this one was named Derek. Everything went the way he directed. He even had a dress for her to wear for the wedding, a lovely blue-green silk that darkened her eyes to emerald, as well as a scrumptious black fake-fur coat, shoes, underwear, even makeup. A hairdresser came to the hospital that morning and fixed her hair in a chic, upswept style. Yes, he had everything under control. It was almost frightening.

He kept his warm hand firmly on her waist as they got the marriage license, then went to the judge's chamber to be married. There, Kathleen got another surprise: the chamber was crowded with people, all of whom seemed ridiculously delighted that Derek was marrying a woman he didn't love.

His mother and stepfather were there; dazedly, Kathleen wondered what his mother must think of all this. But Marcie, as she had insisted Kathleen call her, was beaming with delight as she hugged Kathleen. There were two other couples, two teen-agers, and three younger children. One of the couples consisted of a tall, hard-looking man with graying black hair and a wand-slender woman with almost silver-white hair and glowing green eyes. Derek introduced them as Rome and Sarah Matthews, very good friends of his, but something in his voice hinted at a deeper relationship. Sarah's face was incredibly tender as she hugged him, then Kathleen.

The other couple was Max and Claire Conroy, and again Kathleen got the feeling that Derek meant something special to them. Max was aristocratic and incredibly handsome, with gilded hair and turquoise eyes, while Claire was quieter and more understated, but her soft brown eyes didn't miss a thing. The three youngsters belong to the Conroys, while the two teen-agers were Rome and Sarah's children.

Everyone was ecstatic that Derek was marrying, and Marcie couldn't wait to get to the hospital to visit her new grandchild. She scolded Derek severely for not contacting her immediately, but stopped in midtirade when he leaned down and kissed her cheek, smiling at her in that serene way of his. "I know. You had a good reason," she sighed.

"Yes, Mother."

"You'd think I'd eventually learn."

He grinned. "Yes, Mother."

The women all wore corsages, and Sarah pressed an arrange-ment of orchids into Kathleen's hands. Kathleen held the fragile flowers in shaking fingers as she and Derek stood before the judge, whose quiet voice filled the silent chamber as he spoke the traditional words about love and honor. She could feel the heat of Derek's body beside her, like a warm wall she could lean against if she became tired. They made the proper responses, and Derek was sliding a gold band set with an emerald surrounded by small, glittering diamonds on her finger. She blinked at it in surprise, then looked up at him just as the judge pronounced them man and wife, and Derek leaned down to kiss her.

She had expected the sort of brief, warm kiss he had given her before. She wasn't prepared for the way he molded her lips with his, or the passion evident in the way his tongue probed her mouth. She quivered, her hands going up to grab his shoulders in an effort to steady herself. His hard arms pressed her to him for a moment, then slowly released her as he lifted his head. Purely male satisfaction was gleaming in his eyes, and she knew he'd felt her surprised response to him.

Then everyone was surrounding them, laughing and shaking his hand, and there was a lot of kissing and hugging. Even the judge got hugged and kissed.

Half an hour later Derek called a halt to the festivities. "We'll have a real celebration later," he promised. "Right now, I'm taking Kathleen home to rest. We have to be back at the hospital in a couple of hours to feed Risa, so she doesn't have a lot of time to put her feet up."

"I'm fine," she felt obliged to protest, though in truth she would have appreciated the chance to rest.

Derek gave her a stern look, and she felt inexplicably guilty. Sarah laughed. "You might as well do what he says," the older woman said in gentle amusement. "You can't get around him."

Five minutes later Kathleen was sitting in the Jeep as he expertly threaded his way through the Dallas traffic. "I like your friends," she finally said, just to break the silence. She couldn't believe she'd done it; she had actually married him! "What do they do?"

"Rome is president and CEO of Spencer-Nyle Corporation. Sarah owns Tools and Dyes, a handcraft store. Two stores now, since she just opened another one. Max was a vice president at Spencer-Nyle with Rome, but about five years ago he started his own consulting business. Claire owns a bookstore."

His friends were obviously very successful, and she wondered again why he had married her, because she wasn't successful at all. How would she ever fit in? "And your mother?" she asked quietly.

"Mother helps Whit run his ranch, just across the Oklahoma border. I'd spent Christmas with them, and was on the way back to Dallas when I found you," he explained.

She didn't have anything else to ask him, so silence reigned again until they reached his apartment. "We'll look for something bigger in a few weeks, after your doctor releases you," he said as they left the elevator. "I've shoved things around and made closet space, but feel free to tell me to rearrange anything else you'd like moved."

"Why should I change anything?"

"To accommodate you and Risa. I'm not a bachelor any longer. I'm a husband and a father. We're a family; this is your home as much as mine."

He said it so simply, as if he were impervious to all the doubts that assailed her. She stood to the side as he unlocked the door, but before she could move to enter the apartment he turned back to her and swept her up in his arms, then carried her across the threshold. The gesture startled her, but then, everything he'd done that day had startled her. Everything he'd done from the moment she met him had startled her.

"Would you like a nap?" he asked, standing in the foyer with her still in his arms, as if awaiting directions.

"No, just sitting down for a while will do it." She managed a smile for him. "I had a baby, not major surgery, and you said yourself that I'm strong. Why should I act like a wilting lily when I'm not?"

He cleared his throat as he carefully placed her on her feet. "Actually, I said that you have great muscle tone. I don't believe I was admiring your strength."

Her pulse leaped. He was doing that to her more and more often, saying little things that made it plain he found her desirable, or stealing some of those quick kisses. Five days earlier she would never have found those small advances anything but repulsive, but already a secret thrill warmed her whenever he said or did anything. She was changing rapidly under his intense coddling, and, to her surprise, she liked the changes.

"What are you thinking?" he asked, tapping her nose with a fingertip. "You're staring at me, but you aren't seeing me."

"I was thinking how much you spoil me," she replied honestly. "And how unlike me it is to let you do it."

"Why shouldn't you let me spoil you?" He helped her off with her coat and hung it in the small foyer closet.

"I've never been spoiled before. I've always had to look out for myself, because no one else really cared, not even my parents. I can't figure out why you should be so kind, or what you're getting out of our deal. You've done all this, but basically we're still strangers. What do you want from me?"

A faint smile touched his chiseled lips as he held out his hand. "Come with me."

"Where?"

"To the bedroom. I want to show you something."

Lifting her brows in curiosity at his manner, Kathleen put her hand in his and let him lead her to the bedroom. She looked around. It was a cheerful, spacious room, decorated in blue and white and with a king-size bed. The sliding closet doors were mirrored, and he positioned her in front of the mirrors with himself behind her.

Putting his hands on her shoulders, he said, "Look in the mirror and tell me what you see."

"Us."

"Is that all? Look at yourself, and tell me what I got out of our deal."

She looked in the mirror and shrugged. "A woman." Humor suddenly sparked in her eyes. "With great muscle tone."

He chuckled. "Hallelujah, yes. But that's only part of it. That's not to say I'm not turned on by your fantastic legs and gorgeous breasts, because I am, but what really gets me is what I see in your face."

He'd done it again. She felt her entire body grow warm as her eyes met his in the mirror. "My face?"

One arm slid around her waist, pulling her back to lean against him, while his other hand rose to stroke her face. "Your wonderful green eyes," he murmured. "Frightened and brave at the same time. I sometimes see hurt in your eyes, as if you're remembering things you don't want to talk about, but you don't let it get you down. You don't ask me for anything, so I have to guess at what you need, and maybe I overdo it. I see pleasure when I hold you or kiss you. I see love for Risa, and compassion for the other babies. I've turned your life upside down, but you haven't let it get to you; you've just gone along with me and kept your head above water. You're a survivor, Kath. A strong, valiant, loving survivor. That's what I got out of the deal. As well as a great body, of course, and a beautiful baby girl."

The eyes he had described were wide as Kathleen heard all those characteristics attributed to herself. He smiled and let his fingers touch her lips. "Did I forget to mention what a kissable mouth you have? How sweet and soft it is?"

Her mouth suddenly felt swollen, and her lips moved against his fingers. "I get the picture," she breathed, her heart pounding at her aggressiveness. "You married me for my body."

"And what a body it is." He bent his head to nuzzle her ear, while his hands drifted to her breasts and gently cupped them. "While we're being so honest, why did you marry me? Other than to give Risa all the advantages of being a doctor's daughter."

"That was it," she said, barely able to speak. She was stunned by his touch to her breasts, stunned and scared and shocked, because she was aware of a sense of pleasure. Never before had she enjoyed having a man touch her so intimately. But her breasts were sensitive now, ripe and full of milk, and his light touch seared through her like a lightning bolt.

"Forget about what I can give Risa," he murmured. "Wasn't part of your reason for marrying me because of what I can give you?"

"I . . . I can live without luxury." Her voice was low and strained, and her eyelids were becoming so heavy she could barely hold them open. Her mind wasn't on what she was saying. The pleasure was so intense it was interfering with her breathing, making it fast and heavy. Frantically she tried to tell herself it was only because she *was* nursing Risa that her breasts were so warm and sensitive, and that, being a doctor, he knew it and how to exploit it. He wasn't even touching her nipples, but lightly stroking around them. She thought she would die if he touched her nipples.

"You look gorgeous in this dress, but let's get you out of it and into something more comfortable," he whispered, and his hands left her breasts. She stood pliantly, dazed with pleasure, as he unzipped the lovely dress and slipped it off her shoulders, then pushed it down over her hips to let it fall at her feet. She wore a slip under it, and she waited in a haze for him to remove it, too, but instead he lifted her in his arms and placed her on the bed, moving slowly, as if trying not to startle her. Her heart was pounding, but her body felt liquid with pleasure. She had just had a baby; he knew she couldn't let him do *that* . . . didn't he? But he was a doctor; perhaps he knew more than she did. No, it would hurt too much.

Perhaps he had something else in mind. She thought of his hands on her naked skin, of feeling his big, muscled body naked against her, and a strange excitement made her nerves throb.

Slowly the thought filled her mind that she trusted him, truly trusted him, and that was why she wasn't afraid. No matter what, Derek would never hurt her.

His eyelashes were half-lowered over his eyes, giving him a sensually sleepy look as he slipped her shoes off and let them drop to the floor. Kathleen watched him in helpless fascination, her breath stilling in her lungs when he reached up under her slip and began pulling her panty hose down. "Lift your hips," he instructed in a husky voice, and she obeyed willingly. When the nylon was bunched around her knees, he bent and pressed a kiss to her bare thighs before returning to his pleasant task and removing the garment.

Her skin felt hot, and the bed linens were cool beneath her. She had never *felt* so much before, as if the nerve endings in her skin had multiplied and become incredibly sensitive. Her limbs felt heavy and boneless, and she couldn't move, even when his hands stroked her thighs and pleasure shivered through her. "Derek," she whispered, vaguely surprised to find that she could barely speak; she had slurred his name, as if it were too much effort to talk.

"Hmm?" He was bent over her, the warmth of his body soothing her as he lifted her with one arm and stripped the cover back on the bed, then settled her between the sheets. His mouth feathered over her breasts, barely touching the silk that covered them.

Incredible waves of relaxation were sweeping over her. "You can't make love to me," she managed to whisper. "Not yet."

"I know, sweetheart," he murmured, his deep voice low and hypnotic. "Go to sleep. We have plenty of time."

Her lashes fluttered down, and with a slow, deep sigh she went to sleep. Derek straightened, looking down at her. His body throbbed with the need for sexual relief, but a faint, tender smile curved his lips as he watched her. She had called it "sex" before, but this time she had said "make love." She was losing her wariness, though she still seemed to have no idea why he had married her. Did she think she was so totally without charm or appeal? Did she truly think he'd married her only because of Risa? He'd done his best to convince her that he was attracted to her, but the final argument would have to wait about five weeks longer.

Her thick lashes made dark fans on her cheeks, just as Risa's did. He wanted to lie down beside her and hold her while she slept. He'd known she was tired; since Risa's birth, Kathleen had been sleeping a great deal, as if she had been pushing herself far too hard for far too long. Her body was insisting on catching up on its healing rest now that she no longer had such a pressing need to do everything herself.

The telephone in the living room rang, but he'd had the foresight to unplug the phone by the bed, so Kathleen slept on undisturbed. Quickly he left the room, closing the door behind him, and picked up the other extension.

"Derek, is she asleep yet?" Sarah's warm voice held a certain amusement, as if she had known he would somehow have gotten Kathleen to take a nap by now.

He grinned. Sarah knew him even better than his mother, better than anyone else in the world, except perhaps Claire. Claire saw into people, but she was so quiet it was easy to underestimate her perception.

"She didn't think she needed a nap, but she went to sleep as soon as she lay down."

"Somehow, I never doubted it. Anyway, I've had an idea. Now that I've opened up the other store, I need to hire someone else. Do you think Kathleen would be interested? Erica is going to manage the new store, so I thought Kathleen could work with me, and she'd be able to have the baby with her."

Leave it to Sarah to notice that Kathleen needed a friend, as well as the measure of independence the job would give her while she adjusted to being his wife.

"She'll probably jump at it, but it'll be a couple of weeks before she's able to drive, and at least that long before Risa will be strong enough."

"Then I'll hold the job for her," Sarah said serenely.

"I'm going to remind you of this the next time you accuse me of 'managing' people," he informed her, smiling.

"But hadn't you already thought of it?"

His smile grew. "Of course."

Chapter Six

The day they brought Risa home from the hospital, Kathleen could barely tolerate having the baby out of her sight for a moment. Risa was thirteen days old, and now weighed a grand total of five pounds and six ounces, which was still two ounces short of the five and a half pounds a baby normally had to weigh before Derek would allow it to be released from the neonatal unit, but, as he'd noted before, she was strong. Her cheeks had attained a newborn's plumpness, and she was nursing vigorously, with about four hours between each feeding.

Derek drove them home, then left the Cherokee with Kathleen so she would have a way of getting around if she needed anything, a gesture that eased a worry she hadn't known she had until he gave her the keys. The hospital was only a few blocks away, and the January day was mild, so he walked back.

She spent the day playing with Risa when the baby was awake, and watching her while she slept. Late that afternoon, Kathleen realized with a start that she hadn't given a thought to what she would prepare for dinner, and guilt filled her. Derek had been a saint, coddling her beyond all reason, letting her devote all her time to Risa, doing all the household chores himself, but Risa's homecoming marked a change in the status quo. It had been two weeks since Risa's birth, and Kathleen felt better than she had in years. She was rested, her appetite was better; there was no reason to let Derek continue to wait on her as if she was an invalid. He had given everything, and she had given nothing, not even her attention.

She rolled Risa's bassinet, which she and Derek had bought only the day before, into the kitchen so she could watch Risa while she prepared dinner. The baby slept peacefully, with the knuckles of one fist shoved into her mouth, undisturbed by the rattling of pots and pans. It was the first time Kathleen had cooked, so she had to hunt for everything, and it took her twice as long to do anything than it normally would have. She was relieved when Derek didn't come home at his usual time, since she was running behind schedule, but when half an hour had passed she became concerned. It wasn't like him to be late without calling her himself or having a nurse call to let her know that one of the babies needed him. As short a time as they had been married, she had already learned that about him. Derek was always considerate.

Derek was . . . incredible.

She wanted to give him something, even if it was just a hot meal waiting for him when he came home. She looked at the steaming food, ready to be served, but he wasn't there. She could keep it warming on the stove, but it wouldn't be the same.

Then she heard his key in the door, and she was filled with relief. She hurried out of the kitchen to greet him, her face alight with pleasure.

"I was worried," she said in a rush, then was afraid he would think she was complaining, so she changed what she had been about to say. "Believe it or not, I actually cooked dinner. But I couldn't find anything, and it took me forever to do. I was afraid you'd be home before everything was finished, because I wanted to surprise you."

His eyes were warm as he put his arm around her shoulders and hugged her to him for a kiss. He kissed her a lot, sometimes with carefully restrained passion, and she had stopped being shocked by her own pleasure in his touch.

"I'm more than surprised, I'm downright grateful," he said, kissing her again. "I'm also starving. Where's Risa?"

"In the kitchen, where I could watch her sleep."

"I wondered if you'd spend the day hanging over her bassinet."

"Actually, yes."

His arm was around her waist as they walked into the kitchen. Risa was still asleep, so he didn't disturb her by picking her up. He set the table while Kathleen served the food, then they ate leisurely, one of the few times they'd had a chance to do so. Kathleen knew she was a good cook, and it gave her a great deal of satisfaction to watch Derek eat with evident enjoyment.

When they had finished, he helped her clean up, then, as sort of an afterthought, took a set of car keys out of his pocket and gave them to her. She took them, frowning at him in puzzlement. "I already have keys to the Cherokee."

"These aren't for the Jeep," he explained calmly, going into the living room and sitting down to read the newspaper. "They're for your car. I picked it up on the way home this afternoon."

Her car? She didn't own a car, just the old truck. The truth burst in her mind like a sunrise, robbing her of breath. "I can't take a car from you," she said, her voice strained.

He looked up from the newspaper, his black brows rising in a question. "Is there a problem? If you don't want the car, I'll drive it, and you can have the Jeep. I can't continue walking to the hospital, so buying a car seemed like the logical thing to do."

She felt like screaming. He'd hemmed her in with logic. He was right, of course, but that only made her feel more helpless. She'd felt so proud of preparing dinner for him, the first time she'd contributed anything to their marriage, while he'd stopped on the way home and bought a *car* for her! She felt like an insatiable sponge, soaking up everything he had to give and demanding more just by her very existence, her presence in his life.

Licking her lips, she said, "I'm sorry. I'm just . . . stunned. No one ever bought . . . I don't know what to say."

He appeared to give it thought, but his eyes were twinkling. "I suppose you could do what anyone else would do: jump up and down, squeal, laugh, throw your arms around my neck and kiss me until I beg for mercy."

Her heart jumped wildly. He was as splendid as a pagan god, powerfully built and powerfully male; that wasn't a twinkle in his eyes, after all, but a hard, heated gleam, and he was looking at her the way men have looked at women since the beginning of time. Her mouth went suddenly dry, and she had to lick her lips again.

"Is that what you want me to do?" she whispered.

He carefully put the newspaper aside. "You can skip the jumping and squealing, if you want. I won't mind if you go straight to the kissing part."

She didn't remember moving, but somehow she found herself on his lap, her arms around his strong neck, her mouth under his. He had kissed her so often in the week they'd been married that she'd become used to it, expected it, enjoyed it. In a way his kisses reassured her that she would be able to have something to give, even if it were only physical ease. She couldn't even do that completely, at the present, but at least the potential was there. If he wanted her to kiss him, she was more than willing.

His arms closed around her, holding her to his strong chest as he deepened the kiss, his tongue moving to touch hers. Kathleen felt very brave and bold; she had no idea that her kisses were rather timid and untutored, or that he was both touched and highly aroused by her innocence. He kissed her slowly, thoroughly, teaching her how to use her tongue and how to accept his, holding himself under tight control lest he alarm her.

Finally she turned her head away, gasping for breath, and he smiled because she had forgotten to breathe. "Are you ready to beg for mercy?" she panted, color high in her face.

"I don't know anyone named Mercy," he muttered, turning her face back to his for another taste of her mouth. "Why would I beg for a woman I don't even know?"

Her chuckle was muted by his lips as he turned passion to teasing, kissing her all over her face with loud smacking noises. Then he hoisted her to her feet and got to his. "Wake up the tiny tyrant so I can show you which car is yours," he said, grinning.

Kathleen threw an anxious look at the sleeping baby. "Should we take her out in the cold?"

"Do you want to leave her here by herself? Unless you want to try the key in every car in the parking lot, you have to know which one is yours. It won't take a minute; just wrap her up and keep her head covered. It isn't that cold outside, anyway."

"Are you certain it won't hurt her?"

He gave her a very level look, and without another word she turned to get a jacket for herself and a blanket for Risa. She felt like kicking herself. Did he think she didn't trust him to know what would harm the baby and what wouldn't? He was a doctor, for heaven's sake! He'd taken care of her and Risa from the moment they'd met. She'd really made a mess of it again, kissing him as if she could eat him up one minute, then practically insulting him the next.

When she returned with the blanket, he'd already picked Risa up, waking her, and he was crooning to her. Risa watched him with a ridiculously serious expression, her tiny face intent as she stared up at him, her hands waving erratically. To Kathleen's surprise, the baby was working her rosebud mouth as if trying to mimic Derek's actions. She seemed totally fascinated by the man holding her.

"Here's the blanket."

He took it and deftly wrapped Risa in it, covering her head. The baby began fussing, and Derek chuckled. "We'd better hurry. She won't tolerate this for long; she wants to see what's going on."

They hurried down to the parking lot, and Derek led her to a white Oldsmobile Calais. Kathleen had to swallow her gasp. It was a new car, not a used one, as she'd expected. It was sleek and sporty looking, with a soft dove-grey interior and every optional convenience she could think of. Tears burned her eyes. "I . . . I don't know what to say," she whispered as she stared at it in shock.

"Say you love it, promise me that you'll always wear your seat belt, and we'll take the baby back inside before she works herself into a tantrum. She doesn't like this blanket over her face one bit." Risa's fussing was indeed rising in volume.

"I love it," she said, dazed.

He laughed and put his arm around her waist as the fussing bundle in his arms began to wail furiously. They hurried back inside, and he lifted the blanket to reveal Risa's red, tightly screwed-up face. "Stop that," he said gently, touching her cheek. She gave a few more wails, then hiccuped twice and settled down, once more intently staring up at his face.

He was perfect. Everything he did only compounded the imbalance in the deal she'd made with him. He not only took care of everything, gave her everything, but he was better at taking care of Risa. The parents of his tiny patients all thought he ranked right up there with angels, and all the nurses were in love with him. He could have had anyone, but instead he'd chosen to saddle himself with a . . . a *hick* who didn't know anything but how to work a ranch, and a child who wasn't his. Kathleen felt like a parasite. If nothing else, she could begin to repay him for the car, but to do that she'd have to get a job.

She took a deep breath and broached the subject as soon as he'd laid Risa down. Kathleen didn't believe in putting things off. She'd learned the hard way that they didn't go away; it was better to meet trouble head-on. "I'm going to start looking for a job."

"If you feel well enough," he said absently as he tucked a light blanket around the baby. "You might want to call Sarah; she mentioned something about needing more help in one of her stores."

She'd been braced for objections, but his matter-of-fact acceptance made her wonder why she'd thought he wouldn't like the idea. Then she realized she had expected him to act as Larry would have; Larry hadn't wanted her to do anything except work like a slave on the ranch, and wait on him hand and foot. If she'd gone out and gotten a job, she might have been able to get out from under his thumb before he'd finished bleeding her dry. Derek wasn't like that. Derek wanted her to be happy.

It was an astounding revelation. Kathleen couldn't remember anyone ever going out of their way to give her any sort of happiness. Yet since Derek had appeared in her life, everything he'd done had been with her happiness and well-being in mind.

She thought about his suggestion, and she liked it. She wasn't trained to do anything except be a waitress, but she did know how to operate a cash register; working in a crafts store sounded interesting. She made up her mind to call Sarah Matthews the next day.

When they went to bed that night, Derek practically had to drag Kathleen out of the nursery. "Maybe I should sleep in here," she said worriedly. "What if she cries and I can't hear her?"

Sleeping in the same bed with her without touching her had been one of the worst tortures a man had ever devised for himself, but Derek wasn't about to give it up. Besides, he was ready to advance his plan a step, which wouldn't work if Kathleen wasn't in bed with him. He'd anticipated all her first-night-with-a-new-baby jitters, and set about soothing them. "I bought a baby-alarm system," he said, and placed a small black speaker by Risa's crib. "The other speaker will be by our bed. We'll be able to hear if she cries."

"But she needs to be kept warm—"

"We'll leave the heat turned up, but close the vents in our room." As he talked, he was leading her to the bedroom. He'd already closed the heat vents, and the room was noticeably cooler than the rest of the apartment. Anticipation made his heart beat faster. For over a week he'd let her get used to his presence in the bed; he even knew why she tolerated it. She thought she *owed* it to him. But now he was going to get her used to his touch as well as his presence, and he meant more than those kisses that were driving him wild. He wanted her so much he ached with it, and tonight he would take another step toward his goal.

She crawled into bed and pulled the covers up over her. Derek turned out the light, then dropped his pajama bottoms to the floor and, blissfully nude, got in beside her. He normally slept nude, but had worn the aggravating pajamas since their marriage, and it was a relief to shed them.

The cold room would do the rest. She would seek out his warmth during the night, and when she woke up, she would be in his arms. A smile crossed his face as he thought of it.

The baby alarm worked. A little after one, Kathleen woke at the first tentative wail. She felt deliciously warm, and groaned at the idea of getting up. She was so comfortable, with her head on Derek's shoulder and his arms around her so tightly—

Her eyes flew open, and she sat up in bed. "I'm sorry," she blurted.

He yawned sleepily. "For what?"

"I was all over you!"

"Hell, sweetheart, I enjoyed it! Would you listen to that little terror scream," he said in admiration, changing the subject. Yawning again, he reached out to turn on the lamp, then got out of bed. Kathleen's entire body jerked in shock. He was naked! Gloriously naked. Beautifully naked. Her mouth went dry, and her full breasts tightened until they began to ache.

He held out his hand to her. "Come on, sweetheart. Let's see about our daughter."

Still in shock, she put her hand in his as he gave her a slow, wicked smile that totally robbed her of breath.

Chapter Seven

That smile remained in her mind the next morning as she drove carefully to Sarah Matthews's store, following the directions she'd gotten from Sarah only an hour before. Risa slept snugly in her car seat, having survived the first night in her crib, as well as being tended by her gorgeous, naked daddy. Kathleen had been too stunned to do anything but sit in the rocking chair and hold Risa to her breast. Derek had done everything else. And after Risa was asleep again, Kathleen had gone docilely back to bed again, and let him gather her close to his warm, muscular *naked* body . . . and enjoyed it.

Enjoyed seemed like too mild a description for the way her thoughts and emotions had rioted. Part of her had wanted to touch him, taste him, run her hands all over his magnificent body. Another part of her had panicked; deep in her mind she still hadn't recovered from the brutal, contemptuous way that Larry had humiliated her before walking out.

She didn't want to think about that; she shoved the memory from her mind, and found the blank space it left promptly filled by Derek's sensual, knowing smile. *That was it!* Knowing! He'd known exactly how she had felt!

She found the cozy crafts store easily enough, despite her

lack of total attention to where she was going. There was ample parking, but she carefully parked her spotless new car well away from everyone else, then gathered Risa and the ton of paraphernalia babies required into her arms and entered the store.

There were several customers browsing and chatting with Sarah, as well as each other, but when Kathleen came in a glowing smile lit Sarah's face, and she came right over to take the baby from her arms. "What a darling," she whispered, examining the sleeping infant. "She's beautiful. Missy and Jed will spoil her rotten, just like Derek spoiled them when they were little. I brought Jed's old playpen and set it up in the back, where I used to keep my kids, if you want to put all Risa's stuff back there."

Kathleen carried the bulging diaper bag into the back room, which was a section of the store stocked with doll supplies, as well as a cozy area with several rocking chairs, where Sarah's customers could sit and chat if they wanted. It was the most popular area of the store, and warmer than the front section. A sturdy playpen had been set up next to the rocking chairs, and Kathleen looked at it in bewilderment.

"You drove home to get the playpen after I called you this morning? Who watched the store?"

Sarah laughed, her warm green eyes twinkling. "Actually, I've had the playpen set up for several days. I called Derek the day you were married and told him I needed help here, if he thought you'd be interested."

"He didn't tell me until last night," Kathleen said, wondering if she should be angry at his manipulation, and also wondering if it would do any good.

"Of course not. I knew he'd wait until Risa was home and you were feeling better. But don't let the playpen pressure you into thinking you have to take the job if you don't want it."

Kathleen took a deep breath. "I'd like to take the job. I don't have any training for anything except being a waitress and doing ranch work, but I can work a cash register."

Sarah beamed at her. "Then it's settled. When can you start?"

Kathleen looked around the warm, homey store. This would be a good place to work, even though she hated the idea of leaving Risa during the day. She would have to find a day-care center or a babysitter nearby, so she could nurse the baby during lunch. She supposed Risa would have to get used to a bottle for supplemental feedings, though it made her want to cry to think about it. "I'll have to find someone to keep Risa before I can start," she said reluctantly.

Sarah blinked in surprise. "Why? My babies grew up in this store. That way I could keep them with me. Just bring Risa with you; you'll have more helping hands than you can count. Whenever you feel strong enough to start work—"

"I'm strong enough now," Kathleen said. "After working on a ranch my entire life, I'm as strong as a pack-horse."

"What does Derek think about this?" Sarah asked, then laughed at herself. "Never mind. He wouldn't have told you about the job if he didn't think you were well enough to handle it. It isn't hard work; the only physical labor is putting up stock, and Jed usually manhandles the boxes for me."

Kathleen searched her memory for a picture of Jed, because she knew he'd been at her wedding. "Is Jed the tall, black-haired boy?"

"Yes. My baby's almost six feet tall. It's ridiculous how fast they grow up. Enjoy every moment with Risa, because her babyhood won't last long." Sarah smiled down at the sleeping bundle in her arms, then leaned over and gently deposited Risa in the playpen. "She's gorgeous. Derek must be insuffer-ably proud of her."

It hit Kathleen like a slap that everyone must think Risa was truly Derek's daughter, which would explain why he had hustled Kathleen into such a hasty marriage. Why wouldn't they think it? Risa's hair was the same inky shade as Derek's, as well as her own. She didn't know what to say, yet she knew she had to say something. She couldn't let his friends think he was the type of man who would abandon a woman who was pregnant with his child, not when he had been so good to her, given her so much. In the end, she just blurted it out. "Risa isn't Derek's. I mean, I'd never met him until the day she was born."

But Sarah only smiled her serene smile. "I know; Derek told us. But she's his now, just like you are."

The idea of belonging to, or with, anyone was alien to Kathleen, because she'd never known the closeness. At least, she hadn't until Risa had been born, and then she had felt an instant and overpowering sense of possession. It was different with Derek. He was a man . . . very much so. The image of his bare, powerful body flashed into her mind, and she felt herself grow warm. He had taken her over completely, so in that respect she did belong to him. The odd thing was that she had just sprung to his defense, unwilling to let his friends think anything bad about him. She had felt the need to protect him, as if he belonged to her, and that sense of mutual possession was confusing.

She pushed her thoughts away, concentrating on learning about the shop with the same intensity she'd learned how to be a waitress. As Sarah had said, it wasn't hard work, for which Kathleen was grateful, because she found that she did tire easily. For the most part Risa slept contentedly, whimpering only when she needed changing or was hungry, and occasionally looking around with vague, innocent eyes. It seemed that all the customers knew Derek, and there was a lot of oohing and aahing over the baby.

In the middle of the afternoon, when school was out, Sarah's teenagers came in, with Jed dwarfing his older sister in a protective manner. Missy, who was startlingly lovely, with her father's black eyes and black hair, nevertheless had Sarah's fragile bone structure. When she saw Kathleen, she rushed to her and hugged her as if they were long-lost friends, then breathlessly demanded to know where the baby was. Laughing, Kathleen pointed to the playpen, and Missy descended on Risa, who was just waking from another nap.

Jed watched his sister, and there was something fierce in his own black eyes. "She's crazy about little kids," he said in a rumbly voice, without any adolescent squeak. "She'll be pushing you and Derek out the door every night just so she can babysit." Then he turned and said, "Hi, Mom," as he enveloped Sarah in his muscled arms.

But there was a small frown in Sarah's eyes as she looked up at her son. "What's wrong? You're angry about something." He was too much like his father for her ever to mistake his moods.

"A pipsqueak punk has been hassling Miss," he said bluntly.

"There's nothing to it!" Missy insisted, approaching them with Risa cuddled to her shoulder. "He hasn't really said anything. He just keeps asking me out."

"Do you want to go?" Sarah asked calmly.

"No!" Missy's answer was too swift, denying her casual attitude. "I just don't want to make any big deal about it; I'd be too embarrassed."

"I'll talk to Rome," Sarah said.

"Oh, Mom!"

"I can handle it," Jed said, his voice deadly calm. He reached out and tickled Risa's chin, then deftly scooped her out of Missy's arms.

"Give her back!" Missy said, breathing fire.

They wandered into the back room, still arguing over who would get to hold the baby, and Sarah shook her head. "Teenagers. Just wait," she said with a smile for Kathleen. "Your turn will come."

"Jed's very protective, isn't he?"

"He's just like Rome, but he isn't old enough yet to know how to control all that intensity."

Ten minutes later Missy returned, having regained possession of Risa. Jed had settled down in the back room, watching the portable televison and doing his homework at the same time. "Mom, please don't say anything to Dad about that guy," she began earnestly. "You know how Dad is. You almost couldn't talk him into letting me date, and I *was fifteen!*"

"What guy?" a deep voice asked calmly, and they all whirled to face the newcomer.

"Derek!" Missy said in relief, reaching to give him a hug which he returned, cradling her head against his shoulder for a moment.

Kathleen couldn't say anything; she just stared at him with her tongue glued to the roof of her mouth. The light wind had ruffled his black hair, and with his naturally dark complexion it gave him a raffish look that almost literally stopped her heart. His broad shoulders strained the light jacket he wore, his only concession to the January weather.

Sarah was frowning at him. "Why didn't the bell ring when you came in?"

"Because I reached up and caught it," he answered calmly as he slid his arm around Kathleen's waist and drew her to him. His golden eyes went back to Missy. "What guy?"

"Some scuzzball keeps pestering me to go out with him," she explained. "Jed's gone all macho, and Mom is threatening to tell Dad, and if she does he'll *never* let me date anyone again."

Derek lifted his eyebrows. "Is this scuzzball dangerous?"

An uncertain look flitted over Missy's delicate features. "I don't know," she admitted in a small voice. "Do you think Dad should know?"

"Of course. Why would he blame you for something that isn't your fault? Unless he wants to blame you for being a traffic-stopper."

She blushed, then laughed. "All right. I guess he'll let me go to the prom . . . if I can get a date."

"No boyfriend?" Kathleen asked, having finally found her tongue. Talking to Missy seemed safe enough, though her attention was splintered by the heat of Derek's body against her side.

Missy shrugged. "No one special. They all seem so *young*." With that scathing denunciation of her peer group, she allowed Derek to take Risa from her and went to join Jed.

"You're off from work early." Kathleen finally managed to talk to him, since he had released her when he lifted the baby to his shoulder.

"I'm on call. We have a mother trying to go into labor three months early. If they can't get it stopped, I'll have to be there when the baby is born. I decided to take a break while I can, and see my women."

She felt a pang at the thought that she might not be sleeping with him that night, and even a little jealousy that it was Risa who was cuddled so lovingly on that broad shoulder. Well, he'd made it plain from the start that it was Risa he wanted. Why should she be jealous? Did she want Derek to demand more from her than she could give?

Maybe she just wanted him to demand anything from her, so she would know *what* to give.

"What time do you leave work?" he asked as he checked his watch.

Kathleen looked at Sarah. They hadn't even talked about hours. It had been more like visiting with friends than working, anyway. "Go on," Sarah said, smiling. "You've been on your feet a lot today, and the kids are here to help. See you in the morning at nine. Wait, let me get a key for you." She fetched an extra key from the bottom of the cash register, and Kathleen put it in her purse.

Derek got the blanket and diaper bag from the playpen and wrapped Risa snugly in the blanket. Predictably, she began fussing when her face was covered, and he grinned. "We have to go," he told Sarah as he ushered Kathleen out the door. "Having her face covered makes her mad."

Quickly he carried the baby to the car and strapped her into her seat; she settled down as soon as he whisked the blanket from her face. Then he came around to Kathleen's side and bent down to kiss her. "Be careful on the way home," he said, then kissed her again. "I'll pick up dinner. What do you like? Chinese? Mexican?"

She'd never eaten Chinese food, but she liked tacos. "Mexican?"

He straightened. "I'll get the food and come straight home." Then he closed her door and walked to the Cherokee without looking back.

Kathleen licked her lips as she started the car, savoring the taste of his mouth. She could feel an unfamiliar tightening inside, and her breasts were aching. She glanced at Risa. "Aren't you hungry?"

A tiny fist waved jerkily back and forth as the baby tried to find her mouth with it. She was monumentally unconcerned with her mother's agitation.

Derek was less than half an hour behind her, but they had scarcely sat down to the spicy meal when his beeper went off.

Without hesitation he went to the phone and called the hospital. "All right. I'm on my way."

He barely stopped to snag his jacket on the way out. "Don't wait up for me," he called over his shoulder; then the door closed, and Kathleen sat there with refried beans lumping in her mouth, suddenly tasteless.

The hours passed slowly as she waited for him to come home. Risa was fed and put to bed; then Kathleen tried to become interested in television. When that failed, she tried to read. That was also a dismal failure, and she was furious at herself. She was used to being alone, and had never found it oppressive before. Had she become so dependent on him that she couldn't function without his presence?

At last, disgusted, she went to bed, and her body was tired enough that she went to sleep despite her restless thoughts. When Risa's first hungry cries woke her at one-thirty, the other side of the bed was still empty.

But when she entered the nursery she jumped in surprise, because Derek was sitting in the rocking chair holding the baby while she cried, his hand rubbing her tiny back. There was a terrible emptiness in his eyes that made her hurt, but she sensed that he got some comfort from holding Risa.

"The baby died," he said in a toneless voice. "I did everything I could, but he didn't make it. He wouldn't have had much of a chance even if he'd gone full term; his heart was hopelessly malformed. Damn it to hell and back, I still had to try."

She touched his shoulder. "I know," she whispered.

He looked down at the furious baby, then caught Kathleen's wrist and drew her down on his lap. Holding her against his chest, he unbuttoned her nightgown and bared her breast, then let her take Risa and guide the child's mouth to her nipple. The outraged wails stopped immediately. Derek looked down at the vigorously suckling infant and gathered both mother and child closer to his body, then leaned his head back and closed his eyes.

Kathleen let her head rest on his shoulder, her own eyes closing as she soaked up his warmth and nearness. He needed her. For the first time, he needed her. She knew that any warm body would have done for him right now, but the warm body was hers, and she'd be there as long as her touch gave him comfort. Or maybe it was Risa who gave him comfort, Risa whom he couldn't bear to release. She was a healthy, thriving baby now, gaining weight every day. He had seen death, and now he needed to see life, the precious life of a baby he'd helped into the world.

Kathleen had to bite her lip. Why hadn't he come to their bed? To her? Why didn't he need *her*?

Chapter Eight

Four weeks later, Kathleen could feel a secret smile tugging at her lips as she unlocked the front door and carried Risa inside to her crib. The baby grunted and waved her fists, then broke into a quick, open-mouthed smile as Kathleen tickled her chin. Even Risa was happy, but Kathleen thought her daughter was smiling at the world in general, while *she* had a very personal reason.

The obstetrician had given her a clean bill of health earlier in the day, and since then she hadn't been able to stop grinning. These past four weeks had been almost impossible to bear as she fretted the days away, impatient for the time when she could truly become Derek's wife. He was a healthy, virile man; she'd seen the evidence of it every day, because he had no modesty around her. She couldn't say that she'd gotten used to seeing him nude; her heart still jumped, her pulse still speeded up, she still grew very warm and distracted by all that muscled masculinity. She was even . . . fascinated.

Marital relations with Larry hadn't been a joy. She had always felt used and even repulsed by his quick, callous handling; she hadn't been a person to him, but a convenience. Instinctively, she knew that making love with Derek would be different, and she wanted to experience it. She wanted to give him the physical ease and enjoyment of her body, a deeply personal gift from her to the man who had completely changed her life. Derek was the strongest, most loving and giving man she could imagine, but because he was so strong it sometimes seemed as if he didn't need anything from her, and being able to give him something in return had become an obsession with her. At last she could give him her body, and sexual fulfillment.

He knew of her appointment; he'd reminded her of it that morning. When he came home, he would ask her what the doctor had said. Then his golden eyes would take on that warm intensity she'd seen in them sometimes, and when they went to bed he would take her in his powerful arms, where she felt so safe and secure, and he would make her truly his wife, in fact as well as in name. . . .

Risa's tiny hands batted against Kathleen's arm, jerking her from her exciting fantasy. "If I give you a bath and feed you now, will you be a good girl and sleep a long time tonight?" she whispered to her daughter, smiling down at her gorgeous offspring. How she was growing! She weighed eight pounds now, and was developing dimples and creases all over her wriggling little body. Since she had begun smiling, Missy and Jed were in a constant state of warfare to see who could get her to flash that adorable, smooth-gummed grin, but she smiled most often for Derek.

Kathleen checked her wristwatch. Derek had called the store while she'd been at the doctor's office and left a message with Sarah that he would be a few hours late, so she had time to get Risa settled for the night—she hoped—and prepare dinner before he'd be home. Would candles be too obvious, or would it be a discreet way of letting him know what the doctor's verdict had been? She'd never prepared a romantic dinner before, and she wondered if she would make *a* fool of herself. After all,

Derek was a doctor; there were no physical mysteries for him, and how could there be romance without some mystery?

Her hands shook as she prepared Risa's bath. How could there be romance between them anyway? It was payment of a debt, part of the deal they'd made. He was probably expecting it. The only mystery involved was why she was letting herself get into such a lather over it.

Risa liked her bath and with the truly contrary nature of all children, chose that night to want to play. Kathleen didn't have the heart to hurry her, because she enjoyed seeing those little legs kick. How different things might have been if it hadn't been for Derek! She might never have known the joy of watching her child splash happily in the bathwater.

But finally the baby tired, and after she was dried and dressed she nursed hungrily, then fell asleep at Kathleen's breast. Smiling, Kathleen put her in the crib and covered her with a light blanket. Now it was time for her own bath, so she would be clean and sweet-smelling in case Derek came home in an impatient mood, ready to end his period of celibacy.

She bathed, then prepared dinner and left it warming in the oven until she heard Derek's key in the lock, then hurried to pour their drinks and serve the food while he hung up his coat and washed. Everything was ready when he joined her at the table.

As always, he drew her to him for a kiss; she had hoped he would deepen the kiss into passion, but instead he lifted the warm pressure of his mouth and looked around. "Is Risa already asleep?" He sounded disappointed.

"Yes, she went to sleep right after the bath." She felt disappointed, too. Why hadn't he kissed her longer, or asked immediately what the doctor had said? Oh, he had to know everything was okay, but she still would have liked for him to be a little eager.

Over dinner, he told her about the emergency that had kept him at the hospital. Just when she had decided that her visit to the doctor had slipped his mind and was wondering how to mention it, he asked casually, "Did the doctor release you from her care?"

She felt her heartbeat speed up. She cleared her throat, but her voice was still a little husky as she answered. "Yes. She said I'm back to normal, and in good health."

"Good."

That was it. He didn't mention it again, but acted as if it were any other evening. He didn't grab her and take her off to bed, and a sense of letdown kept her quiet as they read the newspaper and watched television. He was absorbed in a hockey game, which she didn't understand. Football and baseball were more her style. Finally she put down the newspaper she'd been reading and tried one more time. "I think I'll go to bed."

He checked his watch. "All right. I'm going to watch a little more of the game. I'll be there in half an hour."

She waited tensely in the dark, unable to relax. Evidently he didn't need her sexually as much as she'd been counting on. She pressed her hands over her eyes; had she been fooling herself all long? Maybe he had someone else to take care of his physical needs. As soon as the thought formed, she dismissed it. Derek. He had sworn fidelity in their marriage vows, and Derek Taliferro was a man who kept his word.

Finally she heard the shower running, and a few minutes later he entered the bedroom. She could feel the damp heat of his body as he slid between the sheets, and she turned on her side to face him.

"Derek?"

"Hmm?"

"Are you tired?"

"I'm tense more than tired." She could see him staring through the darkness at the ceiling. "It's hard to unwind after a touchy situation like we had this afternoon."

Kathleen moved closer to him, her hands going out to touch his chest. The crisp curls against her palm gave her a funny, warm feeling. Her head found the hollow of his shoulder, and the clean, masculine scent of his skin surrounded her. His arms went around her, the way they had every night for the past four weeks. It was going to be all right, she told herself, and waited.

But he didn't do anything other than hold her, and finally she decided he was waiting for her to give him the go-ahead. Clearing her throat, she whispered, "I . . . the doctor said it's okay for me to . . . you know. If you want to, that is," she added hastily.

Slowly Derek reached out and switched on the lamp, then lifted himself onto his elbow and looked down at her. There was a strange expression in his eyes, one she couldn't read. "What about you?" he asked in that even tone that sometimes gave her chills. "Do *you* want to 'you know'?"

"I want to please you." She could feel her throat closing up under his steady gaze. "We made a deal . . . and I owe you so much it's the least I—"

"You don't owe me a damn thing," he interrupted in a harsh voice she barely recognized as his. Moving abruptly, he rolled away from her and got out of bed, standing there glaring down at her with golden eyes molten with fury. She had never seen Derek angry before, she realized dimly through her shock, and now he wasn't just angry, he was raging. Being Derek, he controlled his rage, but it was there nonetheless.

"Before we got married, I told you we wouldn't make love without caring and commitment; I never said a damned word about keeping a deal or paying a debt. Thanks, sweetheart, but I don't need charity." He grabbed a blanket and slammed out of the bedroom, leaving Kathleen lying in bed staring at the spot where he'd stood.

She shook her head, trying to deal with what had just happened. How had it blown up in her face like that? She had just been trying to give back some of the tenderness he'd given her, but he hadn't wanted her. She began to shake, lying there in the bed that gradually became cool without his body to keep it warm, but it wasn't just the temperature that chilled her. His absence chilled her; she had come to rely on him so much that now she felt lost without him.

She had been fooling herself all along. She didn't have anything to give him, not even sex. He didn't need her at all, despite his words about caring and commitment. She *did* care about him, and she was committed to making their marriage work, but he still didn't want her, not the way she wanted him to. But then, why should he? He was extraordinary in every way, while she was worse than ordinary; she had been, and still was, unwanted.

Her hands knotted into fists as she lay there, trying to control her convulsive shaking. Her parents hadn't wanted her; they had been middle-aged when she was born, and her presence had almost embarrassed them. They hadn't been demonstrative people, anyway, and they'd had no idea what to do with a curious, lively child. Gradually the child had learned not to make noise or trouble, but she had been so starved for love that she'd married the first man who had asked her, and gone from bad to worse, because Larry hadn't wanted her either. Larry had wanted to live off her and the ranch she'd inherited, and in the end he'd bled the ranch to death, then left her because she'd had nothing else to give him.

It looked as if she didn't have anything to give Derek, either, except Risa, but it was Risa he'd wanted, anyway.

Derek lay on the sofa, his jaw clenched and his body burning as he stared through the darkness. Damn, he wanted her so much he hurt, but it was like being punched in the gut for her to tell him he could use her body because she "owed" him! All these weeks he'd done everything he could to pamper her and make her love him, but sometimes he felt as if he were butting his head against a stone wall. She accepted him, but that was it, and he wanted more than mere acceptance . . . so much more.

She watched him constantly, with wary green eyes, as if trying to gauge his mood and anticipate his needs, but it was more the attention of a servant trying to please than that of a wife. He didn't need a servant, but he desperately needed Kathleen to be his wife. He needed her to touch him with the fierce want and love he could sense were bottled up inside her, if she would only let them out. What had happened to her that she suppressed the affectionate side of her nature with everyone except Risa? He'd tried to tell her how much she meant to him without putting a lot of pressure on her, and he'd tried to show her, but still she held back from him.

Maybe he should take what she'd offered. Maybe emotional intimacy would follow physical intimacy. God knew his body craved the pleasure and release of lovemaking; at least he could have that. But she had told him, when he'd asked her to marry him, that things had happened to her, and she might never be able to accept lovemaking again; when he calmed down, he realized that she had come a long way to even be able to offer him the use of her body.

It just wasn't enough. He wanted to erase the shadows from her eyes, to watch her smile bloom for him. He wanted her slim body twisting beneath him in spasms of pleasure; he wanted to hear her chanting love words to him; he wanted her laughter and tenderness and trust. God, how he wanted her trust! But most of all, he wanted her love, with the desperate thirst of a man stranded in the desert.

Everything had always come so easily for him, including women. He'd scarcely reached his teens before older girls, and even women, had begun noticing him. It was probably poetic justice that he had fallen in love with a woman who protected her emotions behind a wall so high he couldn't find a way over it. He had always known what to do in any situation, how to get people to do what he wanted, but with Kathleen he was stymied. Wryly he admitted to himself that his emotions were probably clouding his normally clear insight, but he couldn't detach himself from the problem. He wanted her with a force and heat that obscured all other details.

He was so wrapped up in his rage and frustration that he didn't hear her enter the room. The first he knew of her presence was when her hand touched his shoulder briefly, then hurriedly withdrew, as if she were afraid to touch him. Startled, he turned his head to look at her as she knelt beside the sofa; the darkness hid her expression, but not the strain in her low voice.

"I'm sorry," she whispered. "I didn't mean to embarrass you. I know I'm not anything special, but I thought you might want to . . ." Her voice fumbled to a halt as she tried and failed to find the phrasing she wanted. Finally she gave up and simply continued. "I swear I won't put you in that position again. I'm not much good at it, anyway. Larry said I was lousy. . . ." Again her voice died away, and the pale oval of her face turned to the side as if she couldn't face him, even in the darkness.

It was the first time she'd mentioned her ex-husband voluntarily, and his name brought Derek up on his elbow, galvanized by this abrupt opportunity to learn what had happened between Kathleen and the man. "What happened?" His voice was full of raw, rough demand, and Kathleen was too vulnerable at the moment to deny it.

"He married me for the ranch, so he could live off it without having to work." Her words were almost prosaic, but her voice shook a little in betrayal of that false calm. "He didn't want me, either; I don't guess anyone ever has, not even my folks. But Larry used me whenever he had the urge and couldn't get to town; he said I might as well be some use, because even though I was lousy in bed, I was still better than nothing. Then finally he couldn't get any more money out of the ranch, and he filed for divorce so he could move on to something better. The last time I saw him, he . . . he used me again. I tried to stop him, but he was drunk and mean, and he hurt me. He said it was a goodbye present, because no man would ever be interested in me. He was right, wasn't he?"

Slowly, shakily, she rose to her feet and stood beside him in the darkness. "I just wanted to do something for you," she whispered. "You've done so much, given me so much, and I don't have anything to give you except that. I'd give you my life if you needed it. Anyway, I won't let loving you the way I do embarrass you again. I guess all you want from me is to be left alone."

Then she was gone, walking silently back into the bedroom, and Derek lay on his cold, lonely sofa, his heart pounding at what she'd said.

Now he knew what to do.

Chapter Nine

Kathleen had had years of practice in hiding her emotions behind a blank face, and that was what she did the next day at work. She talked to the customers as usual, played with Risa and chatted with Sarah, with whom she had developed a warm friendship. Being friends with Sarah wasn't difficult; the older woman was serene and truly kind. Within a few days Kathleen had easily been able to see why her children adored her and her big, fierce husband looked at her as if the entire world spun around her.

But Sarah was also keenly intuitive, and by lunchtime she was watching Kathleen in a thoughtful manner. Knowing those perceptive eyes were on her made Kathleen withdraw further inside her shell, because she couldn't let herself think about what a terrible mess she'd made of things.

She couldn't believe what she'd said. It horrified her that she had actually blurted out to him that she loved him, after he had made it so painfully plain that he wasn't interested in her even for sex. She hadn't meant to, but she had only just discovered it herself, and she'd still been reeling from the shock. The hardest thing she'd ever done had been to leave the bedroom that morning; she had steeled herself to face him, only to discover that he had already left for the hospital. Now she had to steel herself all over again, but her nerves were raw, and she knew she couldn't do it if she kept replaying the mortifying scene in her mind.

Sarah placed a stack of embroidery kits on the counter and looked Kathleen in the eye. "You can tell me it's not any of my business if you want," she said quietly, "but maybe it would help to talk about it. Has something happened? You've been so . . . *sad* all day long."

Only Sarah would have described Kathleen's mood as sad, but after a moment of surprise she realized that was exactly how she felt. She had ruined everything, and a choking sadness weighed on her shoulders, because she loved him so much and had nothing to give him, nothing he wanted. Old habits ran deep, and she had just opened her mouth to deny her mood when her throat closed. She had received nothing but kindness and friendship from Sarah; she couldn't lie to her. Tears stung her eyes, and she quickly looked away to hide them.

"Kathleen," Sarah murmured, reaching across the counter to take Kathleen's hands and fold them in hers. "Friends are for talking to; I don't know what I'd have done all these years without my friends. Derek helped me through one of the hardest times of my life, even though he was just a boy then. I would do anything for him . . . and for you, if you'll only tell me what's wrong."

"I love him," Kathleen croaked, and the tears overflowed.

Sarah looked perplexed. "Of course you do. Why is that a problem?"

"He doesn't love me." Hastily she withdrew one of her hands and wiped her cheeks. "He only tolerates me."

Sarah's green eyes widened. "*Tolerates* you? He adores you!"

"You don't understand," Kathleen said, shaking her head in

despair. "You think he married me because he loves me, but he doesn't. He only married me because of Risa, because it was the only way he could get her."

"Derek loves children," Sarah admitted. "He loves all children, but he doesn't marry all their mothers. He may have told you that for reasons of his own, and you may have believed it because it was something you wanted to believe, but *I* don't believe it for one minute. Surely you've noticed by now how he *manages* things; if something doesn't suit him, he works things around until it's just the way he wants it. He talked you into marrying him by using the only argument he thought you'd listen to, but Risa wasn't his main objective; you were."

"You wouldn't say that if you had seen him last night," Kathleen said in bitter hurt. She stared at Sarah, wondering if she should complete her humiliation by admitting everything, only to find that, once she had begun talking, it was more difficult to stop than to go on. "I told him that the doctor had released me—" She drew a deep breath. "I tried to get him to make love to me, and he b-b-blew up like a volcano. He was so angry it scared me."

Sarah's eyes were huge. "Derek? *Derek* lost his temper?"

She nodded miserably. "He doesn't want me, Sarah; he never has. He just wanted Risa. He's practically perfect; all the nurses at the hospital would lie down and let him walk on them if he wanted. He's strong and kind, and he'd done everything he could to take care of us; I owe him so much I can never begin to repay him. I just wanted to give him s-s-sex, if nothing else, but he doesn't even want that from me. Why should he? He can have any woman he wants."

Sarah folded her arms and gave Kathleen a long, level stare. "Exactly," she said forcefully.

Kathleen blinked. "What?"

"I agree with you. Derek can have any woman he wants. He chose you."

"But he *doesn't* want me!"

"In all the years I've known him, I've never seen or heard of Derek losing his temper. Until now," Sarah said. "If he lost his temper with you, it's because you touch him more deeply than anyone else has before. Few people ever cross Derek, but when they do, he never loses his temper or even raises his voice. He doesn't have to; one look from him can shrivel you. His control is phenomenal, but he doesn't have that control with you. You can hurt him; you can make him angry. Believe me, he loves you so much it might frighten you if you knew how he feels. That may be the reason he fed you that line about wanting to marry you so he could have Risa. Risa is adorable, but Derek could have any number of his own children, if children were what he wanted."

"Then why wouldn't he make love to me last night?" Kathleen cried.

"What did he say?"

"He said he didn't need my ch-ch-charity."

"Of course he doesn't. Of all the things Derek would want from you, that wouldn't even be on the list. He wouldn't want gratitude, either. What else did he say?"

Kathleen stopped, thinking, and suddenly it was as if a door opened. "He said something about caring and commitment, but he wasn't . . . I didn't think he meant . . ." Her voice trailed off, and she stared at Sarah.

Sarah gave a very unladylike snort. "Kathleen, you crawl into bed with him tonight and tell him you *love* him, not how grateful you are or how much you owe him. Believe me, Derek will take things from there. He must be slipping, or he'd have handled things better last night. But then, he's never been in love before, so his own emotions are in the way right now."

Sarah's absolute certainty lifted Kathleen out of the doldrums, and for the first time she began to hope. Was it true? Could he possibly love her? She had never been loved before, and it scared her to think that this strong, perfect, gorgeous man could feel the same way about her that she felt about him. She shivered at the thought of putting Sarah's plan into action, because she would be putting her heart, her entire life, on the line, and it would be more than she could bear if he rejected her again.

Her heart was pounding so violently as she drove home that afternoon that she felt sick, and she forced herself to breathe deeply. Risa began fussing, and she gave the child a harried look. "Please, not tonight," she begged in an undertone. "You were so good last night, let's try for an encore, all right?"

But Risa continued fussing, and gradually worked herself into a real fit. Kathleen was only a few blocks from the apartment house, so she kept driving, but her nerves frayed at the effort it took her to ignore her child's crying for even that short time. When she pulled into the parking lot and cut off the motor, she felt a painful sense of relief as she unbuckled Risa from her seat and lifted the baby to her shoulder.

"There, there," she crooned, patting the tiny back. "Mommy's here. Were you feeling lonesome?" Risa subsided to hiccups and an occasional wail as Kathleen gathered everything in her arms and trudged up to the apartment. She had a sinking feeling Risa wasn't going to have a good night.

Just as she reached the door, it opened and Derek stood there. "You're early," she said weakly.

She couldn't read his expression as he reached out to take the baby. "I heard her fussing as you came down the hall," he said, ignoring Kathleen's comment as he put the baby on one shoulder and relieved Kathleen of the diaper bag. "Why don't you take a bath and relax while I get her settled; then we'll have a quiet dinner and talk."

She stepped into the apartment and blinked her eyes in astonishment. What was going on? There was a Christmas tree standing in the corner decorated with strands of tinsel and hand-painted ornaments, while the multicolored lights blinked serenely. There were piles of gift-wrapped boxes under the tree, and fresh pine boughs lent their scent to the air, while glowing white candles decorated the table. An album of Christmas music was on the stereo, sleigh bells dancing in her ears.

The apartment had been perfectly normal when she had left that morning. She put her hand to her cheek. "But this is February," she protested, her voice blank with astonishment.

"This is Christmas," Derek said firmly. "The month doesn't matter. Go on, take your shower."

Then they would talk. The thought both frightened and thrilled her, because she didn't know what to expect. He must have spent most of the day doing this, which meant he had someone covering for him at the hospital. And where had he found a Christmas tree in February? It was a real tree, not an artificial one, so he must have cut it down himself. And what was in those boxes under the tree? He couldn't possibly have found a tree out in the country somewhere, too. It just wasn't possible. Yet it was done.

Despite his instructions to relax, she hurried through her shower, unable to tolerate any delay. When she entered the nursery, Derek had finished bathing Risa and was dressing her. Risa had settled down and was waving her fists around while she gave the little half cooing, half squeaking noises she had recently learned to make. Kathleen waited until she was finished, then took the baby to nurse her. As she settled herself in the rocking chair she looked at Derek uncertainly, wondering if he intended to remain in the room. Evidently he did, because he propped himself against the wall, his warm, golden eyes on her. Slowly she undid her robe and bared her breast, putting Risa to it. The baby's hungry little mouth clamped down on her nipple with comical greed, and for a moment she forgot everything but the baby and this special closeness. Quiet filled the small room, except for the sounds Risa made as she nursed.

Kathleen kept her eyes down, cuddling the baby to her and rocking long after the tugging on her breast had ceased. Derek moved away from the wall, and at last she had to look at him as he leaned down and, with the gentle pressure of one finger, released her nipple from the baby's mouth. "She's asleep," he murmured, and put the baby in her crib. Then he turned back to Kathleen, hot need in his eyes as they moved over her bare chest, and she blushed as she quickly drew the robe around her again.

"Dinner," he said in a strained voice.

Afterward, she was never certain how she managed to eat, but Derek put a plate in front of her and told her to eat, and somehow she did. He waited until they had finished before taking her hand and leading her into the living room, where that impossible Christmas tree still blinked its cheerful lights. She looked at the nostalgic scene, and her throat was suddenly thick with tears. She could never remember truly celebrating Christmas before; it just hadn't been a part of her family's tradition. But she could remember looking at pictures of a family gathered around just such a tree, with love shining in everyone's faces as they laughed and opened gifts, and she could remember the painful longing she had felt for that kind of closeness.

She cleared her throat. "Where did you manage to find a tree?"

He gave her a mildly surprised look, as if wondering why she would think finding a Christmas tree would be difficult for him. "I have a friend who grows them," he explained in that calm manner of his.

"But . . . why?" Helplessly, she gestured at the entire room.

"Because I thought this was what we needed. Why should Christmas be restricted to one certain time, when we need it all the time? It's about giving, isn't it? Giving and loving."

Gently he pushed her down to the floor in front of the tree, then sat down beside her and reached for the closest present, a small box gaily wrapped in scarlet, with a trailing gold ribbon. He placed it in her lap, and Kathleen stared down at it through a veil of hot tears that suddenly obscured her vision. "You've already given me so much," she whispered. "Please, Derek, I don't want to take anything else. I can never begin to repay—"

"I don't want to hear another word about repaying me," he interrupted, putting his arm around her and drawing her close to his side. "Love doesn't need repaying, because nothing can match it except love, and that's all I've ever wanted from you."

Her breath caught, and she stared up at him with liquid green eyes. "I love you so much it hurts," she said on a choked-back sob.

"Shhh, sweetheart," he murmured, kissing her forehead. "Don't cry. I love you and you love me; why should that make you cry?"

"Because I'm not good at loving. How could you possibly love me? Even my parents didn't love me!"

"That's their loss. How could I *not* love you? The first time I saw you, there in that old truck with your arms folded around your stomach to protect your baby, staring at me with those frightened but unbeaten green eyes, I went down for the count. It took me a little while to realize what had happened, but when I put Risa in your arms and you looked at her with your face lit with so much love that it hurt to look at you, I knew. I wanted that love turned on me, too. Your love is so fierce and strong, sweetheart; it's concentrated from being bottled up inside you all those years. Not many people can love like that, and I wanted it all for myself."

"But you didn't know me!"

"I knew enough," he said quietly, looking at the tree, his eyes calm with a deep inner knowledge few people ever attained. "I know what I want. I want you, Kathleen, the real you. I don't want you tiptoeing around, afraid of doing something in a different way from how I would have done it. I want you to laugh with me, yell at me, throw things at me when I make you mad. I want the fire in you, as well as the love, and I think I'll lose my mind if you don't love me enough to give it to me. The last thing I've ever wanted is gratitude."

She turned the small box over and over in her hands. "If loving is giving, why haven't you let me give anything to you? I've felt so *useless*."

"You're not useless," he said fiercely. "My heart wouldn't beat without you. Does that sound useless?"

"No," she whispered.

He put one finger under her chin and tilted her face up, smiling down into her eyes. "I love you," he said. "Now you say the words back to me."

"I love you." Her heart was pounding again, but not because it was difficult to say the words; she barely noticed them. It was the words he'd said that set the bells to ringing. Then she realized bells really were ringing; the stereo was now playing a lilting song about Christmas bells. A smile tilted her lips as she looked at the twinkling lights. "Did you really do this just for me?"

"Umm, yes," he said, bending his head to nuzzle her ear and the curve of her jaw. "You gave me the most wonderful

Christmas of my life; I got you and our pretty Christmas baby all at one time. I thought I should give you a Christmas in return, to show you how much you mean to me. Open your present."

With trembling fingers she removed the wrapping paper and opened the small box. An exquisite gold locket in the shape of a heart gleamed richly on its white satin bed. She picked it up, the delicate links of the chain sliding over her fingers like golden rain.

"Open it," Derek whispered. She used her nail to open it, and found that it wasn't just a simple two-sided locket. There was more than one layer to it. There was room for two pictures; then she lifted a finely wrought divider section and found places for two more. "Our picture will go in the first section," he said. "Risa's will go in the side opposite ours, and our future children will go in the second section."

She turned the locket over. On the back was engraved, You already have my heart; this is just a symbol of it—Your loving husband, Derek.

Tears blurred her eyes again as she clasped the locket in her hands and lifted it to her lips.

He put another, larger, present in her lap. "Open this one," he urged gently.

There was a small white card uppermost in the box when she opened it. She had to wipe the tears from her eyes before she could read the inscription: *Even during the night, the sun is shining somewhere. Even during the coldest winter, somewhere there are bluebirds. This is my bluebird to you, sweetheart, so you'll always have your bluebird no matter how cold the winter.* Inside the box was a white enamel music box, with a small porcelain bluebird perched on top, its tiny head tilted upward as if ready to sing, the little black eyes bright and cheerful. When she lifted the top, the music box began to play a gay, tinkling tune that sounded like bird song.

"Open this one," Derek said, putting another box in her lap and wiping her tears away with his hand.

He piled box after box in her lap, barely giving her time to see one present before making her open another. He gave her a bracelet with their names engraved on it, a thickly luxurious sweater, silk underwear that made her blush, bunny-rabbit house shoes that made her laugh, perfume, earrings, record albums and books, and finally a creamy satin-and-lace night-gown that made her breath catch with its seductive loveliness.

"That's for *my* enjoyment," he said in a deep voice, looking at her in a way that made her pulse speed up.

Daringly, she lifted her head, stopping with her lips only inches from his. "And for mine," she whispered, almost pain-fully eager to taste his mouth, to know the feel of his body on hers. She hadn't known love could feel like this, like a powerful river flooding her body with heat and sensation and incred-ible longing.

"And yours," he agreed, taking her mouth with slow, burning expertise. Her lips parted for him automatically, and his tongue did a love dance with hers. She whimpered, her hands going up to cling behind his neck as blood began to pound in her ears. She felt warm, so warm she couldn't stand it, and the world seemed to be tilting. Then she felt the carpet under her, and Derek over her. His powerful body crushed her against the floor, but it wasn't painful. His mouth never left hers as he opened her robe and spread it wide, his hands returning to stroke slowly over her bare curves.

Never in her imagination or her dreams had she thought loving could be as wildly ecstatic as Derek showed her it could. He was slow, enthralled by her silken flesh under his hands, the taste of her in his mouth, the restless pressure of her legs around his hips as she arched mindlessly against him,

begging for something she didn't fully understand. Her innocence in that respect was as erotic to him as her full, love-
stung lips or the entranced look in her green eyes. He took
his time with her despite his own agonizing tension and need,
soothing her whenever some new sensation startled her. Her
rich, lovely breasts were his, her curving hips were his, her
silken loins were his.

She cried out, her body surging against his as he finally
entered her with exquisite care, making her his wife in flesh
as well as heart. They loved each other there on the carpet,
surrounded by the presents he'd given her and the strewn, gaily-
colored paper that had wrapped them. The candles burned with
their serene white flame, and the joyously colored lights on the
tree cast their glow on the man and woman, twined together in
the silent aftermath of love.

Derek got to his feet and lifted Kathleen in his muscled arms.
"I love you," she whispered, lacing kisses across his throat.

Her naked body gleamed like ivory, with the lights casting
transparent jewels across her skin. He looked down at her with
an expression that both frightened and exalted her, the look of a
strong man who loves so much that he's helpless before it. "My
God, I love you," he said in a shaking voice, then glanced around
the living room. "I meant to wait; I wanted you to wear the gown
I bought you, and I wanted you to be comfortable in our bed."

"I'm comfortable wherever you are," she assured him with
glowing eyes, and he cradled her tightly to him as he carried
her to their room. Most of his presents to her remained on the
living room floor, but two were clutched in his hands: the heart-
shaped locket, and the bluebird music box. The winter was cold,
but not her heart. She would always have her bluebird and the
memory of her first real Christmas to keep her warm while her
bluebird sang her lover's song to her.

A Note from the Author

In my family it takes us three days to properly celebrate Christmas. My husband, Gary, and I both come from large families, and when it's taken into account that some branches of our families have lived in this area for at least a hundred and fifty years, that gives us an enormous extended family of aunts, uncles, cousins, nieces, nephews, in-laws, and out-laws, as well as kissing cousins of various degrees. It takes a while to see that many people.

Gary and I begin small, with our own immediate family: Mike, Donna, Tammy, Jeff and Mark. Seven people isn't bad; this is our quiet time. From there, though, it quickly becomes something resembling either a three-ring circus or a riot.

Then we move on to our parents' houses. Christmas with my parents involves only three generations under one roof, and even though it's an army, it's a small one. The toddlers are thoroughly petted and spoiled, and everyone keeps an eye out because the babies could get lost in the sea of discarded wrapping paper.

At Gary's parents' we have our four-generation Christmas celebration. Forget about chairs; just find a bare spot on the floor to sit and don't dare get up. Bribe people to bring things to you. If a trip to the bathroom is necessary, you've lost your place to sit. Kids are everywhere, like puppies, their excited laughter adding to the din of conversation. We all eat so much we just want to lie down, but there isn't room. Actually, we start munching on the extra goodies like stuffed dates and the shrimp ball as soon as we get there. I usually don't get hungry again until about the twenty-seventh.

Just thinking about it makes me smile. Merry Christmas.

Lynda Howard

About the Author

Linda Howard is the *New York Times*–bestselling romance and suspense author of *Up Close and Dangerous, Drop Dead Gorgeous, Cover of Night, Killing Time, To Die For, Kiss Me While I Sleep, Cry No More,* and *Dying to Please.* She is a charter member of Romance Writers of America and in 2005 was awarded their Lifetime Achievement Award. Howard lives in Gadsden, Alabama, with her husband and two golden retrievers. She has three grown stepchildren and three grandchildren.

LINDA HOWARD

FROM OPEN ROAD MEDIA

OPEN ROAD

INTEGRATED MEDIA

OPEN ROAD
INTEGRATED MEDIA

Find a full list of our authors and
titles at www.openroadmedia.com

FOLLOW US
@OpenRoadMedia